STORIES

JOHN SHEA

STORIES

acta
PUBLICATIONS

STORIES
Written by John Shea

Edited by Gregory F. Augustine Pierce
Cover design by Tom A. Wright
Text design and typesetting by Patricia A. Lynch

Published by ACTA Publications, 5559 W. Howard Street, Skokie, IL 60077-2621, (800) 397-2282, www.actapublications.com

Library of Congress Number: 2008931389

ISBN: 978-0-87946-374-8

Printed in the United States of America by Versa Press

Year: 15 14 13 12 11 10 09 08
Printing: 10 9 8 7 6 5 4 3 2 1

♻ Cover printed on Rainbow 17 from Ecological Fibers, Inc.
   Text printed on 30% post-consumer waste paper

Table of Contents

Sources of Stories / 7

Publisher's Note / 11

Introduction / 13

All I Want Is What Is Mine / 17

The Antique Watch / 37

The Belt Buckle / 41

The Cigar Smoker / 45

Cro-Magnon Popcorn / 53

The Daughter of Christmas / 57

A Down-and-Out Disciple Meets His Match / 63

The Evangelizers on the Beach / 77

The Father of Ice Cream / 81

Forbidden Fruit / 89

Goin' Fishin' / 95

The Higher Math of Sr. Imelda / 103

"How Come I Feel So Bad?" / 109

The Kaleidoscope / 113

The Kid with No Light in His Eye / 123

"Let Them Be Who They Will Be" / 135

Lord Love a Duck / 147

Making a Home for Spirit / 155

Martha the Good / 161

The Mother of Soda Bread / 169

My Father's Wealth / 175

My Mother's Best Putt / 183

Paint the Other Side / 189

The Phone Call / 197

The Rock / 203

"Scaring Ain't So Bad" / 209

Shame on Al / 213

Shenanigans at Cana / 217

The Shoelace / 223

Star Gazer / 229

Twenty into Fifty Goes a Hundredfold / 233

Waking Up on Christmas Morning / 241

Why Bother? / 247

The Woman and the Kid in Lincoln Park / 255

The Woman at the Well / 261

Sources of Stories

THE SPIRIT MASTER
(Thomas More Press, 1987)
The Cigar Smoker
Cro-Magnon Popcorn
The Daughter of Christmas
A Down-and-Out Disciple Meets His Match
The Father of Ice Cream
"Let Them Be Who They Will Be"
Lord Love a Duck
Martha the Good
The Mother of Soda Bread
Paint the Other Side
The Phone Call
Shame on Al
Shenanigans at Cana
Star Gazer
Twenty into Fifty Goes a Hundredfold

THE LEGEND OF THE BELLS
(ACTA Publications, 1997)
The Antique Watch
Paint the Other Side
The Rock
The Woman and the Kid in Lincoln Park

GOSPEL LIGHT
(The Crossroad Publishing Company, 1998)
Forbidden Fruit

ELIJAH AT THE WEDDING FEAST
(ACTA Publications, 1999)
The Belt Buckle
The Couple Planting a Tree
The Evangelizers on the Beach
The Higher Math of Sr. Imelda
"How Come I Felt So Bad?"
My Father's Wealth
My Mother's Best Putt
"Scaring Ain't So Bad"
The Shoelace

CHRISTMAS PRESENCE
(ACTA Publications, 2002)
The Kaleidoscope

AN EXPERIENCE NAMED SPIRIT:
SPIRITUALITY AND STORYTELLING
(Liguori Publications, 2004)
All I Want Is What Is Mine
The Boy Turned Man
Goin' Fishin'
The Kid with No Light in His Eye
Why Bother?
The Woman at the Well

THE SPIRITUAL WISDOM OF THE GOSPELS FOR
CHRISTIAN PREACHERS AND TEACHERS – YEAR A
(Liturgical Press, 2004)
Making a Home for Spirit

STARLIGHT
(ACTA Publications, 2006)
Waking Up on Christmas Morning

To Those Who Have Listened

and

To Those Who Will Read

Publisher's Note

I t's not often that we get to publish a book with just the name of the author and a one-word title. When it comes to *John Shea: Stories*, however, what else do we need?

Shea has been making up and telling and writing down stories all his adult life. And they are not just any stories. They are stories of the spirit, stories of the unexpected, stories of incarnation, stories that get at the deepest questions of what life is all about.

His stories are "Christian" in the most fundamental meaning of that word. That is, they are inspired by the author's lifelong love affair with the Jesus story and the holy scriptures that tell it. That is why each of the stories in this book has a Gospel quote at the beginning. Not because the stories are a reflection on or retelling of a particular Bible passage but because they "hint at the ultimate meaning of what follows," as Shea says in his Introduction.

ACTA Publications has been honored to publish many of Shea's stories over the years, both in book form and as audio and video programs. He has told literally thousands of stories over the years "which are not recorded in this book," as the evangelist John might have said. We decided to limit this volume to those stories that are "pure Shea," that is, stories that he composed himself, not the stories of others, the traditional folk tales, or the spiritual teaching stories of the world's religious traditions which he often tells.

The thirty-five stories here have appeared in previous Shea books, some going back twenty-five years, but they are brought together for the first time. So pull up a chair to the precipice of the sacred and let John Shea tell you some stories about how we get there.

Gregory F. Augustine Pierce
Co-Publisher
ACTA Publications

Introduction

There is no neat way to classify these stories.

Some came from my own experiences. But more often than not, when I told them, I disguised them in one way or another.

Some began as one-line observations that jumped out at me from random conversations or stunned me as I turned the pages of a book or article. For reasons I do not know, my imagination fancied the words and spun them into characters, dialogues and plots.

Some are riffs on well-known Biblical narratives, mainly Gospel stories. I had meditated on them for so long, I could not resist adding to their music. Before I knew it, the story had gone well beyond its sacred precincts.

Some were situations people innocently told me about, commenting that I might be able to use them in a talk or homily. They knew the appetite of public speakers for material. Their sketchy situations became story seeds and, through conscious and unconscious nurture, gradually grew into trees—and I hoped at least some of the birds of the air might find a home in their branches.

But, as varied as these stories are in origin and inspiration, they share some common features.

They all have been told, either in whole or in part, before they were written down. They were not written and then read, a standard way for stories to be received by listeners. They had an oral origin that was gradually refined and finally stabilized in a written form. The written form is the same story as the spoken form, but it is not simply a matter of typing on a page what my voice said. As they took written form, there were subtle changes in phrasing and sometimes significant developments. In written form they found their way into books of stories and reflections like *The Legend of the Bells* and *Elijah at the Wedding Feast* and into books of theology and spirituality like *An Experience of Spirit*, *The Spirit Master*, and *Starlight*. In this book they are gathered together in one place and the dedication page reflects this spoken-written history: To Those Who Have Listened and To Those Who Will Read. The recipients of the stories, either as listeners or readers or both, are the ultimate unifiers of the collection.

Therefore, it is natural that when I see these stories in print, I think of the times I told them. When I am telling a story, I can feel the flow between myself and the listeners. We both are attentive and invested in what is unfolding. The story becomes a commonly shared world. What happens to the characters in the story is important, and, to some extent, what is happening to them is also happening to us. Even wilder, things are happening to us that we cannot imagine. The story is creating outcomes we cannot predict or control. I believe it was F. Scott Fitzgerald who said, "Pull your chair up to the precipice and I will tell you a story." In telling and listening to stories there is that dual quality of alertness and peril. It is quite a kick.

They also share in common a spiritual ambition. Despite the secular cast of my mind that comes unsolicited as a gift of American culture, I have never been able to shake the intuition that a spiritual dimension permeates who we are and what we do. However, it is not easily available to conventional consciousness. As Lao Tzu suggested, it lingers like gossamer, barely hinting at existence. But, on occasion, it manifests itself in our physical and social life. It lifts up our tired bodies and suffuses our routine with adventure. If we are alert to this shining of the Spirit through the flesh, we can be illumined, comforted and challenged in ways we never suspected. The stories seek to express and communicate this type of manifestation.

The spiritual intent of the stories is evoked by the Gospel quotations that serve as a headline. Many novels, short stories, and poetry collections begin with quotations. I always take them as hints to the ultimate meaning of what follows. No matter what the readers may take from what they are reading, the author has provided a thread through the labyrinth. The quotation is not meant as a constraint but as a guide. When I reached for guides, I dipped into the Gospels. It is the well I always drink from.

Therefore, these stories are humble servants (as is their author), waiting upon Spirit and remembering the paraphrased words in one of Flannery O'Connor's short stories, "When the sun strikes the trees a certain way, even the meanest of them sparkle."

All I Want Is What Is Mine

But there are many other things that Jesus did.
If every one of them were written down,
I suppose that the world itself could not contain
the books that would be written.
—John 21:25

I never saw him. I never heard him. I never touched him. But there were those who did. And they told others, who told others, who told others still, who eventually told me. And now, in my turn, I tell you so that you, too, can tell others. And so, you see, there will never be an end to it.

E ventually, they all came to Jesus. Even at night they sought him out. Perhaps better said, especially at night they sought him out.

He would be seated on the ground before a fire, teaching and telling tales. His disciples would be close around him, a bit officious, warding off the very people Jesus wanted near. They were always saying, "The Master thinks that…" only to find out that the Master did not think that. Usually, in fact, he thought the opposite. But they never seemed to learn. That is why down to this day we call them disciples.

The influential would often drop by. They would stand, their robes unsoiled, at the outer rim of the fire's light. Their arms would be folded across their chests in grim listening. None could mistake that they were men of seriousness. When they spoke, their right arms would shoot out like a dagger thrust, then return to the sheath of their sides. Jesus always said, "Come closer, we can barely see you." They never did.

The adulators would also crowd around the fire. "Hello, Jesus, remember me?" They would sit cross-legged, head in hands, their mouths open, their ears eager for every syllable. They would listen for hours on end, not understanding a word.

They would listen for hours on end, not understanding a word.

Of course, the ill were there. The sick flocking to the physician, as he would say. A man with an arm as gnarled as a washed-up branch on a beach. A blind woman feeling for the warmth of a fire she could not see. Sorrowing parents with a crazed son, tied round with ropes, his lips white with froth. The obligatory pallet bearers with paralyzed friend. It was quite a scene. It would be hard to say who, at one time or another, didn't make it.

And, of course, troubles. Always troubles. It was like each person was a secret tale of tears, and with him they had a chance to cry. A son who would not obey; a daughter who ran away. A husband who would not come to bed; a wife who would not talk at meals. A tax-collector without a heart; a priest without a soul. A land which would not yield wheat; a tree which would not bring forth figs. A lake without fish; a home without heat. Too little bread; too much wine. Troubles—and him there in the middle, the fire leaping, casting a circle of light in the dead darkness of the Galilean night.

Once, while Jesus was speaking, a young man pushed through the outer edge of the crowd and moved toward him. Although there was an urgency to his stride, there was no loss of poise or presence. He was robed in linen and purple. As he passed the fire, the signet ring on his right hand gleamed. He was obviously heir to more than the wind. All eyes followed him, including those of Jesus who had fallen silent the moment the man appeared.

He found a place to the right of Jesus and sat down. Then they found each other's eyes. "Yes?" said Jesus.

"Rabbi," the young man's voice was as imposing as his walk, "make my brother divide the inheritance with me. I want my share of the money."

"You are lucky enough to have an inheritance?" said Jesus. "I myself have nowhere to lay my head." He was playing with him.

The young man did not want to play. "I'm not an heir yet. My brother refuses to comply. All the rabbis since Moses have insisted that if one of the sons wants it, the inheritance must be divided. All I want is what is rightfully mine; what is rightfully mine is all I want. Tell him to give it to me."

Now Jesus did not want to play. "Friend, who made me a divider between you and your brother?" Then he looked beyond the young man at the gathering of people. "Am I now divider among you all?"

"Rabbi," explained the young man, "the more which I want is coming to me." His voice was as logical as a ledger. "I do not ask for what is not mine. Neither do I ask you to be a divider between me and my brother. I will be the divider. All I ask of you is to command the division."

All who heard him were impressed with the legitimacy of his claim and the clarity of purpose that informed his speech. All except one.

Jesus turned away from the petition and stared into the fire. He did not speak.

Now we Christians mourn because so many of the

words of Jesus were lost. The words of the Word of God were carried away with the wind. But, Christians, trade them all, trade them all for the thunder of one of his silences.

When he finally turned back to the young man, the story was already on its way. "Once there was a rich farmer," said Jesus.

"He was well into his middle years. Not like you," Jesus gestured to the almost-heir, "still in the vigor of youth. He was rounded from the good life, as fat as a banquet calf. Not like you, lean and muscular."

One evening, while he was at table with his family and friends, the foreman of his farm suddenly stood at his door. Fearing something was wrong, he went outside to see him. "The wheat has sprouted in a strange way, tripling what we had expected," said the foreman.

"I must see this," said the farmer. He had a servant bring him a torch, and leaving his family and guests without a word, he and the foreman went out into the fields. The blaze of the torch pushed back the darkness enough for the farmer to see the superabundance. Somehow the seed had multiplied. Surplus was everywhere.

"The earth is generous, my lord," said the foreman. "You are the heir of a miracle."

But the farmer did not hear him. Thinking to himself, having only himself to think to, he thought, "I need bigger barns to hold my surplus wheat."

"Tear down the barns and build bigger barns," commanded the farmer.

"Master," said the foreman timidly, "if we do that, the wheat already stored will be lost."

"Of course," muttered the farmer. "How foolish of me! All this wheat muddled my thinking. For a moment I lost my perspective. Keep the barns we have. What I need is more. Build more barns to house the surplus that is rightfully mine."

Thinking to himself, having only himself to think to, he thought, "How will I keep all this extra from the others who are not me?"

When the farmer returned to the house, his guests and friends were gone. His family had retired without kissing him.

The months that followed found the farmer anxious. Thinking to himself, having only himself to think to, he thought, "How will I keep all this extra from the others who are not me?"

So he hired carpenters to build special locks for the barns. When they came to his land and saw the incredible abundance of wheat almost white for harvest, they told the farmer, "You are blessed."

"Will the locks be strong enough?" the farmer asked.

There was no celebration on the final day of harvest. As soon as the workers were finished, the farmer dismissed them. He wanted to secure the locks himself. When the last wooden bar slid into place, the farmer, thinking to himself, having only himself to think to, thought, "Now I will never be hungry again."

Now Jesus stared directly at the young man who was nothing like the farmer. "He never was hungry again. That night he died. Now tell me what will happen to all the surplus that was rightfully his? Whose inheritance will it be now?"

For the length of time it takes to rub mud on the eyes of the blind; for the length of time it takes to push spittle into the ears of the deaf; for the length of time it takes to breathe life into the mouth of the dead, there was silence.

"Then you won't tell my brother," the young man finally blurted out.

"No!" said Jesus. It was the only way he could say, "Yes!"

The young man stood and began to break through the circle of people, shoving them aside as he went. Jesus' eyes never left the boy as he moved farther and farther away. Finally, he pushed past the outer edge. He was gone as abruptly as he came. The night swallowed him.

We might want to know more but more is not ours to know. The record is silent. Except that sometimes when Jesus was restless, he would tell his disciples, "Stay here by the shore of the sea. I will go to the mountains." Or he would say, "Stay here in the village. I will walk the desert." When he would return to tell them what the mountains whispered or what secrets the desert could not keep, he would often ask them:

"While I was gone." And his voice would trail off.

"If when I was away was there perhaps any word?" and his eyes would search the sky.

"Did you hear anything?" and he would fumble with words like a man afraid to ask but hoping too much not to ask.

"Is there any news about the young man who, more than anything else, only wanted what was rightfully his?"

Peter hated to see Jesus like this—so tentative and beaten, not cutting his losses like a sensible man and moving on, but worrying about what was over. So, as he tried so often to do, Peter consoled Jesus.

"Why bother?" Peter said. "He is gone. You have us."

The disciples were already seated around Jesus. They joined with Peter in telling him to forget the young man. The rich are like that, they assured him. The young man may walk away, but they would always be there. There was no need for him to brood. It was natural that some would not understand and reject his offer. He should not expect everyone to be receptive. Did he himself not say that some seed falls by the side of the road and is lost?

Jesus waited till they were finished. Then the Son of the Father spoke.

Once there was a certain man who had two sons. The younger son was a bird. He rode every wind, and played his life out against the sky where all could see him climb and fall. The older son was a rock, centuries could tear at him and he would withstand. He was as secret as soil. He made few mistakes, and those he made, he did not advertise. In his heart the father delighted in them both.

He would watch them in the field. The younger son, stripped to the waist, would recklessly gather what he could. The row of wheat he harvested looked like the wind had reaped it. A village could eat for a week on what the ground still held. When he reached the end of a row, he would turn and yell, "I'm finished." Then he would run back to where his father was and say, "Look at all this wheat."

"Yes" the father said.

The older son, properly covered, moved over the field meticulously, like a man sensing a treasure was about to be unearthed. He missed nothing; lost nothing. When he finished, he walked silently back to where his father watched. "We still have the crops on the west to bring in," he said.

"Yes," the father said.

The day the father knew would come came. The younger son approached him. "Father, give me my share of the inheritance. All I want is what is rightfully mine." So the father called both his sons together, sat them down at table, and divided his money between them. When he was finished, he asked, "Is this fair?"

The older brother thought to himself, "If I was going, there would not be these tears."

They both nodded.

"I have no more," the father said. "All I have is yours."

Within a few days the younger son gathered together his belongings and inheritance and set out for a far country. At his departure the father threw his arms around him and wept. "O Father," the younger son said. He was embarrassed by this display of affection; his arms never left his sides. The older brother, who was watching this farewell, thought to himself, "If I was going, there would not be these tears."

Jesus stood now and walked around the circle of his disciples, touching each of them.

In the far country, this younger brother was no Joseph. He was without his cloak in many a house, but it was not to walk naked and noble away from the lust of some Potiphar's wife. This younger brother was no Jacob who could mastermind two sheep into a herd. Under the guidance heir, the inheritance dwindled and disappeared. And when a famine covered the land, the king did not make him the overseer of the granaries, but a small farmer made him keeper of the pigs. And his fall was so great that he would have eaten the slop they fed the swine, but the farmer would not let him.

In this condition the son who once cried "See how much wheat we have!" cries "Who will feed me?" He knows. In his Father's house there is food, but he will have to beg for it. In his mind he writes the word of his disgrace. "Father, I have sinned against heaven and thee. Do not take me back as a son but only as a hired hand." With only these words in his mouth, he moves toward home.

Jesus finished the round of his disciples. He had touched them all. He had missed none of them. He sat down again and waited a long time before he continued.

On the hill beside his home, the father waits. He has been there before. He sees his son coming from a distance, and lifting his robes above his knees, he runs to greet him. The servants who are out in the field watch the old man running past them, his breath short, his eyes never wavering. By the time the younger son sees him, the father is on top of him. He embraces his son and weeps down his neck.

"Oh Father," said the son, his arms never leaving his side.

"Bring the robe," said the father. The servants had gathered around.

"I have sinned."

"Bring the ring."

"Against heaven."

"Bring the sandals."

"And against thee."

"Kill the fatted calf."

"Do not take me back."

"Call in the musicians."

"As a son."

"My SON," and these words the father whispered into his ear, "was dead and has come back to life."

"But as a hired hand."

"My SON was lost and now is found."

The party had no choice but to begin.

"Go," said the older brother, "and tell my father I will not party with him."

The older brother was out in the fields. He had worked late as usual. The sweat of the endless day dripped down his face. When he drew near the house, he stopped at the top of the hill. He heard the sounds of rejoicing and dancing. He grabbed one of the servant boys and asked him what was happening. The boy said, "Your younger brother has returned, and his father has killed the fatted calf and is rejoicing."

"Go," said the older brother, "and tell my father I will not party with him."

The servant boy entered the house and within moments the father came out of his home. He pulled his robe above his knees and, out of breath but with his eyes unwavering, climbed up the hill to where his older son was standing.

"O my beloved son!" the father said, and embracing him, he wept upon his neck.

"All these years," said the older brother, his arms at his sides, "I have slaved for you."

"O my beloved son!" said the father. And with the sleeve of his robe, he wiped the sweat of the slave from his son's forehead.

"And you have never given me a calf so that I might party with my friends. But this son of yours comes groveling home having squandered your inheritance with whores, and for him, for him, you kill the fatted calf."

"O my beloved son!" said the father a third time. "You have been with me always, and all I have is yours. But if any son of mine was lost, surely this feast will find him. If any brother you know is dead, surely this party will bring him to life." Then the father kissed both of the earth-hardened hands of his oldest son.

Suddenly the father was old. He was a tired man. He turned and moved back down the hill. When he reached the bottom, he noticed his younger son had come out of the house. The robe he had put on him had slid off one shoulder. The ring he had given him had been too large for his starved finger and barely clung to the knuckle. The leather of the new sandals had already cut a ridge on his ankles. The father looked back up at his oldest son. He seemed to be frowning. The sweat of the slave was still on him. Between them both stood the father.

The music from the party (that none of them were attending, at the moment) drifted from the house and hung in the air between them. Suddenly the father was no longer tired. He lifted his robes, and there between the son on the hill and the son outside the house, the joy of his heart overflowed into his feet. In broken rhythm he began to dance, hoping the music he could not resist would find the hearts of the two brothers and bring his sons, his true inheritance, back to him.

Jesus now looked at Peter and said, "Why bother?"

The man who once saw in the flesh of his friend the radiance of God saw it again. "Because a man always has two sons," Peter said.

Jesus lept up. A great cry of joy ran out from him. And from where Peter sat it seemed his hands touched the sky, and his outstretched arms were wide enough to welcome everyone.

These are two of the stories I must tell you because they have been told to me. And now that you have heard, you must tell others. But if all the forests that ever were cut down and all the wood from those forests turned to paper and all the quills that ever were were dipped into all the ink that ever was and those quills put into the hands of all the scribes that ever wrote, even then not all that Jesus Christ did and said while he lived among us in the flesh could be recorded. But I tell you these things so that we may have life.

The Antique Watch

"A man found a treasure buried in a field."
—*Luke 19:10*

For twenty years, I was a teacher. At Christmastime, it was the custom at the school where I taught for all the kids to bring gifts.

After about the third year, I could name the gift by the size of the box it came in. Whenever my students would come up with long, flat boxes, I would know they were handkerchiefs. Since thank-you notes were not expected, I would take these long, flat boxes and just throw them in my closet unopened. Then, as I needed a handkerchief, I would open a box and take one out. I always had more boxes than I needed handkerchiefs.

One time I went into my closet, took out a box, and opened it. Instead of a handkerchief, there was an antique pocket watch. All this time, I possessed an antique pocket watch and I didn't know it.

The Belt Buckle

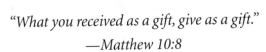

"What you received as a gift, give as a gift."
—*Matthew 10:8*

It happened in Oklahoma City when I was a young man, fresh on the speakers' circuit. I had just finished my talk, and people were coming up to ask me questions or point out things I should have said.

An old Native American man—a Cherokee, I suppose—suddenly stood in front of me. He had a large and elaborate belt buckle in his hands. It was a swirl of multicolored beads. If they formed a pattern, I couldn't detect it.

"Please accept this gift," he said.

I was a little taken aback, but I had a quick response: "Thank you. It's beautiful. But I can't accept it."

"Why not?" he asked with a puzzled look.

I pointed to the expanse beneath my chest. "Well, would you want to call attention to this stomach with a large, beautiful belt buckle?" I laughed.

The man did not smile. He simply extended the belt buckle again. "Please accept this," he said again.

"It's too expensive," I said. This was probably closer to the truth of why I said no. I was always taught not to take expensive presents from people. The belt buckle was hand-crafted and had a look of elegance about it.

"You know," the old man said, "you can give it to someone else."

I accepted the belt buckle.

Eventually, I followed the old man's advice and gave the belt buckle to someone else, a student whom I thought had made excellent progress.

The student said he couldn't take it.

I told him the story of how I had received it, and then he took the belt buckle with a knowing smile. Although we did not discuss it, I am sure he knew the gift was to be given away. It was not a possession but a mission.

Today, tonight, tomorrow, soon...someone is moving toward you with a beautiful beaded belt buckle. He or she will not take "no" for an answer.

The Cigar Smoker

"Whoever welcomes a child such as this, welcomes me."
—*Mark 9:27*

The Kingdom of God is like a cigar smoker without his cigar.

The cigar smoker was giving a workshop in Los Angeles. It began in glory and ended in humiliation. At the close people were grumbling and his departure was more in the nature of an escape. But as the cab dragged through traffic to the airport, he thought to himself, "If only I can get to the airport, get on the plane, nurse a double martini, eat whatever lousy food the airline is serving, and smoke my cigar, everything will be all right." For this was many years ago when cigar smoking on airplanes was allowed.

For the first time in three days there were no hitches. He got to the airport, got on the plane, and plunked himself down in an aisle seat in the smoking section.

Next to him in the middle seat was a little girl, around four years old. She had with her everything little girls carry on airplanes—a half-eaten bag of Fritos, a coloring book with a box of broken crayons, and a doll, mussed from too much hugging and squeezing. In the window seat sat the little girl's mother.

Los Angeles, as usual, was socked in, a thick mixture of fog and smog. As the plane left the ground, it entered the thick, grey clouds. The cabin darkened. But as the plane climbed, the cabin grew progressively lighter until the dazzling moment when the plane broke out of the clouds into the sun.

The captain turned off the no-smoking sign. The woman in the window seat lit up a cigarette. When the cigar smoker looked over and saw her, his heart sank. As she exhaled the smoke, she waved her hand back and forth in front of her mouth. The smoke wafted upward and drifted toward the front of the cabin.

The cigar smoker instantly knew what this meant. This woman was going to smoke her cigarette, but there was going to be no smoke in the little girl's eyes. But the cigar smoker also knew that when he lit up his cigar, smoke would swirl through the cabin, infiltrate the cockpit, and seep out into the universe. And if he lit up his cigar, the little girl would be engulfed in smoke. She would cough her pathetic little-girl cough. People would stare at him angrily. He would be the bad guy of all time.

The cigar smoker folded his arms and allowed the injustice full reign over his soul. His thoughts boiled.

Did he not get a seat in the smoking section? He did.

Did they allow you to smoke cigars in the smoking

section? They did.

Did he need a cigar? Oh sweet Jesus, he needed a cigar.

Would he be allowed to smoke a cigar? He would not.

He sank sullenly into the seat and entertained the idea of locking the little girl in the washroom.

The woman in the window seat finished her

He sank sullenly into the seat and entertained the idea of locking the little girl in the washroom.

cigarette and said to the little girl, "Jennifer, come here." She helped Jennifer slide over and sit on her lap. "Jennifer," the mother instructed her, "look at the clouds."

Jennifer looked out the window of the airplane and looked down at the clouds. The little girl immediately began to sob and repeat in a frightened voice, "We're upside down! We're upside down!"

The cigar smoker turned toward the noise and coolly observed the little girl's panic. He thought to himself, "All her life this little kid has been standing on the ground looking up at the clouds. Now she is over the clouds looking down. She naturally thinks she is upside down." But he decided that it was not his place to say anything.

Jennifer's mother was the soul of logic. She explained to her, "We are on an airplane, Jennifer. When you are in an airplane, you go up in the air. When you go up in the air, you go over the clouds. So you see we are not upside down. We are right side up." And then from the mother's mouth came a conclusion that she was obviously not prepared to admit but which she could not avoid. "The clouds are upside down."

To which Jennifer replied, her sobs deepening, "We're upside down! We're upside down!"

The mother pressed the button for the cabin attendant; and down the aisle came a trained and confident stewardess, prepared for any eventuality.

She leaned over the cigar smoker and said in a voice of syrup to the little girl, "What's your name?"

"Jennifer," the girl whimpered.

"What's the matter Jennifer?"

"We're upside down."

"No we're not, honey," the flight attendant assured her.

Then she talked about her experience of flying and that sometimes she gets afraid too, but that really there is nothing to worry about because the captain knows what he is doing, and what she finds often helps is some Coca-Cola and some peanuts, and that she was going to get some and bring them back to her, and then she would see that there was no reason to cry.

The cabin attendant retreated down the aisle, smiling.

Jennifer sobbed, "We're upside down! We're upside down!"

Jennifer's mother, leaving reason, resorted to discipline. She picked the little girl off her lap and planted her firmly back in the middle seat. "Sit there and be good," she warned.

Jennifer sat there, holding her thin knees and making soft crying noises that anyone with an ear to hear could pick up.

The cigar smoker heard. He leaned over to the little girl and said, "Jennifer, you are upside down!"

The little girl looked up at him in grateful recognition.

"But it's O.K.," said the cigar smoker. "It's O.K."

Jennifer climbed over the arm of the seat and sat in the

cigar smoker's lap. And for a moment before her mother could rescue her, for one dazzling moment comparable to when an airplane breaks out of the darkened clouds into the sun, the cigar smoker knew he really didn't need the cigar.

Cro-Magnon Popcorn

"A good measure, pressed down,
shaken together, running over,
they will pour into the folds of your garment."
—*Luke 6:38*

With the possible exception of Leonardo da Vinci Airport in Rome during a ground crew strike, the popcorn counter at the Varsity Cinema five minutes before the beginning of *The Return of the Jedi* is the most hassled place on earth.

Behind the twenty-foot plate glass counter scurries a teenage girl. She is alone, struggling to respond to fifty pressing patrons. She is racing up and down the counter—diving for Raisinettes, dipping to fill a popcorn box, jamming a cup under the Coke dispenser. Her long blond hair is tied in a ponytail; when she turns suddenly to fill an order, it lifts off her back like a kite.

Waiting in line is Robert, known affectionately to the other members of the football team as Cro-Magnon Man. When he finally reaches the front line of customers, he speaks two words. They sound as if they were shouted into a canyon. "Large popcorn."

The frazzled girl scoops up the popcorn into the tub box, slams it on the counter, and moves on. But with the hard contact on the counter the popcorn, which appeared to fill the box, caves in. There had been a false bottom of air. Only three-quarters of a box of popcorn stares up at Cro-Magnon Man.

A sound emits from Robert, a primitive, guttural cry of pain as if the tusk of a wild boar had torn into his leg.

The patrons turn in terror, sure the end is upon them. The counter girl stops in her tracks, looks back, and immediately sizes up the situation. She grabs the popcorn scoop, loads it with popcorn, and upturns it over Robert's box. The popcorn fills the box, brims over, and spills onto the countertop.

The patrons turn in terror, sure the end is upon them.

"Here, monster!" says the girl, laughing.

Robert utters a second sound, a low purr of pleasure as if someone infinitely larger than he was had reached down and petted him.

The Daughter of Christmas

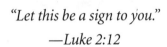

"Let this be a sign to you."
—Luke 2:12

The Christmas tree is a towering beauty. It drips with tinsel, bursts with ornaments, and is strung with technicolor lights. Under the tree is a large crib set. Joseph and Mary, Wise Men and shepherds, sheep and camels—all have their eyes on the baby Jesus. The eyes of baby Jesus, however, are looking up and out into the living room, where the entire family has gathered to exchange gifts.

A present is passed to the uncle first. Over the years the family has learned that Christmas is more pleasant if he is first to open a gift.

"Mine?" he grins and attacks the box. He wrestles the brightly colored wrappings free, muscling them into a sphere which he basketballs toward the trash bag. Then he forces the box open and sizes up the white shirt and red tie.

"Needed," is his one-word appraisal. "Who do I have to thank for this?" The card was lost in the carnage.

Next a gift arrives at the lap of his niece who is twelve. She opens the card and reads each line carefully, as painstakingly as a Biblical scholar.

"Oh, thank you!" she exclaims. It is from her grandmother. In one bound she is across the room with a flurry of kisses and a hug.

"You better check it out first," her uncle suggests. "You never know. It could be socks."

She does not hear him. She is back at the box. As carefully as a mother unwraps the blanket in which a baby is cradled, she unfastens and folds the green paper.

"Going to save it?" her uncle chides. The ceremony is tedious to him. His eye drifts to a big box near the door.

As carefully as a mother unwraps the blanket in which a baby is cradled, she unfastens and folds the green paper.

"Green is one of my favorite colors and grandma knew that when she picked it out. Besides, you can always use pretty paper."

The box reveals a green sweater with a sky of white stars on the upper half from shoulder to shoulder.

The uncle watches his niece shriek with delight, cover her grandmother with a second round of kisses, and disappear into her room.

"Could we continue opening the presents while she is trying on the sweater?" the uncle said, and gave an exasperated and adult shrug of his shoulders like a man who has been burdened with too much common sense.

But before anyone could answer his plea for speed, his niece returned wearing her new sweater and spun around for all to see.

"O thank you," she said. It sounded like a song.

No one noticed the Christmas tree.

A Down-and-Out Disciple
Meets His Match

Then their eyes were opened and…
he vanished from their sight.
—Luke 14:31

It was a wind-blasted winter evening, close to midnight, in the year of Our Lord Nineteen Hundred and Eighty-Six, and the doors of the apartment were locked. Inside, the disciple was eating popcorn and riffling through the gospels. He was reading at top speed, flipping pages, hoping a word, a sentence, a story would make him stop. He was looking for something, but he wasn't sure what it was.

Suddenly Jesus appeared and sat down in the chair opposite him. The disciple blanched. He shook, rubbed his eyes, looked away, and looked back. Jesus stubbornly stayed put. Finally Jesus said, "Got anything to eat?"

"I get it," said the disciple. "That's what you did after you rose. When the disciples thought you were a ghost, you asked for something to eat. It reassured them you were real."

"I was hungry. What is this stuff?"

"Popcorn." The disciple passed the bowl over to Jesus. "Try some, Lord," he said; and the words sounded absolutely ludicrous. He consoled himself with the thought that he didn't say, "Mister Lord."

Jesus took one piece of popcorn and looked at it as though he were examining a diamond with an eyepiece.

"Wonderful shape," Jesus said, "and each one is just a little different. I like them."

The disciple became a little uneasy. He had never heard popcorn referred to as "them." And how did he know he liked them if he hadn't tasted them?

Jesus put one piece in his mouth and chewed it carefully for close to a minute. The disciple grabbed a handful.

"Not enough salt," Jesus finally said.

"Salt is not good for you," warned the disciple.

"I was always one for a lot of salt," said Jesus. "Hey!" Jesus raised his finger in the air like he was about to give a teaching. "Has anyone tried putting butter on this stuff?"

"It's been done. But butter's not good for you either."

"You are a very careful person," said Jesus.

"Thanks," said the disciple. "Here, have some more." The disciple raised the bowl of popcorn off the table and offered it to Jesus.

"No thanks."

"You are the only person I know who can eat only one piece of popcorn and stop."

"Of course. I'm God," Jesus said, and laughed.

The disciple did his best to chuckle.

"How come when YOU eat popcorn," Jesus said as he stroked his chin, "you try to get as much into your mouth as possible, and it spills out, and you have to pick it off your shirt, and put it back in your mouth?"

"Oh God, I knew this was going to happen."

"Why does everybody say that when I'm around?" asked Jesus, a bit irritated. "What did you know was going to happen?"

"You notice everything and make remarks."

"You don't like to be noticed?"

"As a matter of fact, I don't."

The disciple closed his eyes. When he opened them, Jesus was still there, and smiling.

"Why did you come?"

"To teach you how to eat popcorn." Jesus looked pleased with himself.

The disciple looked down at the bowl of popcorn on the table. "Are you going to toy with me?" he said, angrily.

"I am not toying with you. I always come to seek what is lost; and when people are searching through my story at midnight like it was a medicine cabinet, it is usually a sign they are lost."

"Like hell I'm lost!" the disciple shouted.

"Like hell you're not!" Jesus shouted back.

Their eyes locked. The disciple was the first to look away.

"It's a mild case of mid-life crisis. I'll be over it in a couple of months." The disciple gave a "what can I tell you" shrug of his shoulders.

"Is that what they are calling temptation these days—mid-life crisis?"

The disciple laughed in spite of himself.

Slowly Jesus reached over to the bowl of popcorn, took one piece, and popped it into his mouth. Jesus' obvious enjoyment made the disciple shake his head.

"Even God can't eat only one piece of popcorn," said the disciple.

"Especially God," said Jesus. "Try some."

The disciple instinctively took a handful of popcorn, but then let some fall back into the bowl. He put the pieces in his mouth two or three at a time.

When both of them had finished chewing, Jesus said in a very gentle voice, "You have been with me now a long time, and you are wondering whether it is all worth it. You've got your hand on the plow and your head on backwards."

"It used to be easy," the disciple said, rummaging his memory. "You died for me, and I owed you, so I signed up. But, now I ask, who asked you to die for me?"

"You died for me, and I owed you, so I signed up. But, now I ask, who asked you to die for me?"

"My father, of course."

"I never asked you to."

"You wouldn't. You're the type who doesn't like to be noticed. You would rather die yourself."

The disciple's head snapped straight back like someone had just pounded a fist into his chin. Before he could respond, Jesus had a suggestion.

"I think you follow me because you like my teachings."

"You've got to be kidding. Some of them make sense.

But most of them I don't get, and all of them are too hard."

"Name one."

"Anyone who lusts after a woman in his heart has already committed adultery."

"Name another."

The disciple laughed. Jesus laughed at the disciple's laughter.

"You know, one of the worst times," Jesus' voice was mellow and reflective, "was after my father raised me. Mary went to the tomb and found two angels but not my body. The angels asked, 'Woman, why are you weeping?' She tells them she doesn't know what has happened to my body and it is driving her crazy with grief. ALL THE TIME I'M STANDING RIGHT BEHIND HER. She turns and looks right at me. I decide to ape the angels. 'Woman,' I say, 'why are you weeping?' Then I point to myself like a little boy on stage and say in gentle joyous mockery, 'Who is it that you are looking for?' It was a little showy, but I was happy to see her.

"But she says, 'Sir.' She calls me, 'Sir.' That 'Sir' killed me a second time. I realized that she didn't recognize me. She thinks I'm the gardener, and wants to know if I have any information about the whereabouts of my own body. I cry out in her pain and mine, 'Mary!' And she knows me. It was only when I said her name that she found my body. That's what I meant about lust. You know what I mean?"

"No."

"Think about it."

"Tell me about your father."

"Love to. I was floating on my back in the Sea of Galilee. The water was holding me up effortlessly. It was buoying me up and stretching me out and, as I later reflected, getting me ready to receive. I was looking straight up into the sky. No clouds. Just a blue so deep it was hard to look at. When suddenly the sky fell into me. I felt like infinite azure. It was my father playing around. Have you ever felt like infinite azure?"

"Sometimes."

"Have I ever made you feel like infinite azure?"

"Not in a long time."

"How about finite aquamarine?"

"Don't mock me!"

"A definitely limited indigo?"

"Cut it out!"

"Look!" Jesus grabbed his disciple's shoulders and looked into his eyes. "You are drowning in self-pity. Play with me. I can't take dismal disciples."

The disciple put his head down. He did not look at Jesus.

After a couple of minutes, Jesus asked, "What are you thinking about?"

"You tell me. I thought you could read hearts."

"Only when the wind is right. What's going on?"

"Why don't you just go away?"

"I can't. I told you. I came to seek what is lost. I'm the Messiah."

"The scholars say you didn't use titles for yourself."

"You read too much and you are trying to get me off the subject like that woman I met by the well."

"What's the subject?"

"You."

"Well, did you use titles?"

"Is there any mule in your lineage? O.K. I'll tell you. Back in those days, people were overeager to believe in messiahs, so I didn't mention it. Today, people are overeager not to believe in messiahs, so I say it. I offended them by not saying it, and I see I embarrass you by saying it."

"You do not. I am a believer."

"You are an embarrassed believer."

"Well, wouldn't you be?" The disciple stood up and walked away from the table. "Here I am, a modern person, looking to a first century Jew for the meaning of life? There are a lot of other models around."

"Someone a little more in step with the times?" asked Jesus.

"Right!"

"Like Lee Iacocca."

"You're mocking me again."

"You are thinking of divorcing me quietly, aren't you?"

"It has crossed my mind."

"My friend, you need more chutzpah. Blessed are those who are not embarrassed of me."

The disciple sat back down at the table. There were no words for a long time.

Then Jesus said, "There was a bank robber who planned a heist for a long time. He had worked out the details and was ready to go. But when he got to the bank teller's window, he suddenly panicked and asked directions to the washroom."

"Hah! You are saying I can't carry through with what I set out to do."

"I'm saying risk the salt on the popcorn."

"Jesus," the disciple said in an exasperated voice, "I'm going to lay it on the line. You walk too fast: I can't keep up."

"Better to be out of breath behind me than ahead of everyone else."

"Better to be out of breath behind me than ahead of everyone else."

"I want a more moderate master so I can be a better disciple."

"You are a perfect disciple—you cannot receive my death, you cannot live up to my teachings, my father scares you, and you do not know how to eat popcorn."

"That may be accurate but it is hardly perfect."

"My friend, that is the way of the earth beyond the earth. Why live out of something as small as you are? Love me because I am large enough to betray. But I do not think you are happy in the land of mercy."

"God, you are a bittersweet experience."

"There is no lie in me."

"Why do you say things so harshly?"

"Peter used to say that I was the only one who could say, 'God loves you' and get everybody mad."

The disciple laughed. So did Jesus.

"You laugh at the right places," said Jesus. Then suddenly he asked, "So, are you going to stick around?"

"Where will I go? You have the words of eternal life."

"No fair stealing Peter's lines."

"Will YOU stick around with someone like me?" The disciple sighed like some great buildup of pressure had been released.

"Is that what this is all about?" asked Jesus. "You know all things, you know that I love you."

"No fair stealing Peter's lines. Why did you say that?"

"When Peter said it to me, it blew me away. I hoped it might do the same for you."

"But I don't know everything."

"You know enough."

"I know that even when I want you to go away, I don't want you to go away."

"East of Eden we call that love," said the master, and tears ran freely down his face.

In imitation of his master, the disciple cried.

For a long time there were no words, only the silence of communication.

"You know," Jesus finally said, "after Lazarus came back to life, he told me that what woke him up in the tomb was the sound of my tears."

"I can believe it," said the disciple.

Jesus smiled and reached for a third piece of popcorn. The disciple also took a piece. Jesus closed his eyes to savor better. The faithful disciple did likewise. When the disciple opened his eyes, Jesus was gone. But there was such an inner, incredible lightness to his being, that the disciple knew where he had vanished to.

The Evangelizers at the Beach

They were on the road to Jerusalem.
Jesus was ahead of them…
and those who followed were afraid.
—*Mark 10:32*

Years ago, I was lying on the North Avenue beach in Chicago in the late afternoon. The sun was beating down on me when all of a sudden a shadow blocked the light. For a moment I thought it was a passing cloud, but then I opened my eyes and there were two young people standing over me.

They were well-washed and groomed. He had on a white shirt and a tie, and she wore a blouse and a skirt. They were carrying their shoes, and they each had a Bible in hand.

They looked down on me and asked, "Do you know the Lord Jesus as your personal savior?"

I looked up and answered without missing a beat, "Unfortunately, yes."

The Father of Ice Cream

"What father among you will give his son
a snake if he asks for a fish,
or hand him a scorpion if he asks for an egg?"
—*Luke 11:11*

Tom, eleven, was the first in the door at 31 Flavors. He announced to everyone in the store, "I get the window on the way back."

Alice, the oldest at thirteen, followed. She was somewhere between dolls and nylons and she looked like she would rather be anywhere but where she was. Janet, who was nine, was shoved through the door by Jeff, who was aggressively eight. Next came the biggest of the group, a man by the name of Daddy, who was holding the hand of the smallest of the group, a boy by the name of Paul.

They all lined up in front of the plate glass wonderland. "Whatever you want," said the father. His arms spread out, indicating all thirty-one flavors.

"I want a scoop of rocky road and licorice in a cup," grinned Jeff, the eight-year-old.

"Daddy, Daddy, Daddy!" Janet, the nine-year-old, was sputtering. "That's what I was going to get. I told Jeff in the car that I was going to get that. That's why he got it."

"Janet, I'm sure they have enough rocky road and licorice for two," the great mediator assured her. She glared at her father.

Meanwhile Tom had conned the teenage girl behind the counter into giving him a taste of pralines 'n' cream and double chocolate. He was now pushing along into banana fudge and pineapple swirl.

"Tom!" shouted his father. Tom backed off and returned the little pink tasting spoon to the girl. His father said only one word, but the communication was unmistakable. They had had the conversation before.

"Daddy," said Alice in a refined voice, "I'll have two scoops of lime sherbet in a cup." She got her sherbet and drifted away from her embarrassing family toward a group of teenagers in the corner.

Paul, the five-year-old, had said, "Daddy," three times and tugged vigorously on his father's pants before he looked down. "I want bubblegum peppermint."

"Don't get the bubblegum peppermint," coaxed his father. "You like chocolate chip."

"I want bubblegum peppermint." Paul's voice moved toward tears.

"O.K. But you are going to finish it," said the father, doing his imitation of a stern parent.

The father turned back to Janet, who was pouting in the corner. "What will you have, honey?"

"Vanilla." Her voice was as cold as the ice cream.

Jeff said, "Boy, this rocky road and licorice is good."

"Jeff!" said the father. It was the same one word conversation he had had with Tom. Jeff walked away.

The father bent down for a private conversation with Janet. "Janet, honey, don't cut off your nose to spite your face. Get the rocky road and licorice."

She looked at her father as if he were the dumbest man on the face of the earth. He knew nothing about life. "Vanilla in a plain cone," she said adamantly. She would not be denied the wrong done to her.

Janet looked at her father as if he were the dumbest man on the face of the earth. He knew nothing about life.

Tom was pacing up and down in front of the glassed-in choices.

"You'll have to make up your mind," said his father.

"O.K. I'll have a hot fudge banana split with four scoops of ice cream—chocolate, double chocolate, chocolate chip and chocolate ripple."

"No extra nuts?" suggested his father.

"Extra nuts!" said Tom excitedly.

"And two maraschino cherries for my son," added the father.

"I don't like this bubblegum peppermint," came a voice from the floor.

"Give it to me, Paul," said the father. "And give him a scoop of chocolate chip in a plain cone." The teenage girl behind the counter hurried it up.

The father licked the bubblegum peppermint. He didn't like it either.

Then, out of the wealth of his pockets, Daddy paid for it all.

The father was herding his children out the door when Alice, his oldest, said, "Daddy, I'm going to stay with these kids I met."

He looked over at the teenagers in the corner with that steely parental appraisal that withers all wrongdoing.

"Be home by five." He was startled by the tenderness in his voice.

From outside came Tom's voice. "I said I have the window on the way home."

The father turned immediately and pushed out the door, for his children needed him.

Forbidden Fruit

"Why do you think these things in your heart?"
—*Mark 2:8*

Every night, when my father came home from work, he would do the same thing. I was six, and every night I watched him.

We lived on the second floor of a two-flat. I could hear him coming up the stairs before I could see him. When he came through the door, I was there. He would pat me on my crew cut and take off his hat and plop it on my head. It would slide forward over my eyes and sideways over my ears. All this was done while he was walking, while he was making his way toward the bedroom, while I was following, pushing the hat back to see.

My father was a policeman. He carried a gun in a holster at his hip. It was not slung low like the cowboy gunslingers in the serials I saw at the West End Theater on Saturday mornings. It rode waist-high. Once, as we were walking toward the bedroom, I asked him if he could draw fast enough with the gun that high.

"It's not like that," he said.

On the top shelf of the closet in my mother and father's bedroom was a wooden safe. My father had it made to size, and it was a snug fit, perfect height and perfect depth. On the shelf next to the safe was a key. With his back to me, my father would open the closet door, take the key off the shelf, and open the safe. Then he would take off his belt and holster and take the gun out of the holster. The holster and belt would be rolled up and stuffed way back in the safe. Then he would open the cylinder of the gun. The bullets would slide out into his free hand. He would put the bullets in a dish that was inside the safe. I could hear them clinking as they rolled and settled into place. Then he would put the gun in the safe, lock it, and put the key on the shelf. This is what he would do every night when he came home—as I watched.

One night after he had put the bullets in the dish, he turned and walked over to me.

One night after he had put the bullets in the dish, he turned and walked over to me. He was holding the gun by the barrel. Without saying anything, he offered me the handle. I took it. Its heaviness surprised me. My arm fell to my side. I quickly heaved my arm up. It was all I could do to hold it upright. My father took it out of my hand, opened the cylinder, and rolled it.

"This is where the bullets go," he said. "When you pull the trigger, the chambers move."

He paused.

"Do you want to play with it?" he finally said.

I nodded.

He gave me the gun. "Don't pull the trigger."

I went to the window and pointed the gun at the two-flat next door.

I looked at my father. He was watching me, but he said nothing.

I went over to the bed, hid behind it, then popped up and aimed.

My father said nothing.

I put the gun in my pocket and jerked it out. Fast-draw.

My father said nothing.

I put the gun in my belt and pulled it out. Fastdraw.

My father said nothing.

I lay on the floor and took aim. Gunshot sounds came out of my mouth.

My father said, "Are you done?"

I nodded and handed him the gun. He turned and

went to the safe. As he was locking the gun away, with his back to me, he said, "There—now you don't have to be figuring out how to get it all the time."

Goin' Fishin'

They caught so many fish
that the nets were beginning to break....
—Luke 5:6

It is known by everyone who cares to know that the Lord Jesus and St. Peter used to repair to the local tavern after a hard day of ministry to break bread and drink wine together.

On a certain rainy night, St. Peter turned to the Lord Jesus and grinned. "We're doing real good."

"We?" said the Lord Jesus.

Peter was silent. "All right, you're doing real good," he finally said.

"Me?" said the Lord Jesus.

Peter pondered a second time. "All right, God's doing real good," he finally admitted.

But the Lord Jesus saw how reluctant St. Peter was to admit the source of all goodness. He laughed and hit the table with glee.

It was the laugh that got to St. Peter. He pushed his face toward Jesus and blurted out, "Look it! I was somebody before you came along. You didn't make me. I know now everybody says, 'There goes the Lord Jesus and his sidekick St. Peter. Jesus cures them and Peter picks them up.' But it wasn't always that way. People knew me in my own right. I was respected and looked up to. They would say, 'There goes Peter, the greatest fisherman in all of Galilee.'"

"I heard that you were a very good fisherman, Peter," said the Lord Jesus who was always ready to praise.

"You're damn right I was. And tomorrow I am going to prove it. We are going to go fishing, and you will see how the other fishermen respect me and look to my lead."

"I would love to go fishing, Peter. I have never been fishing," said the Lord Jesus who was always looking for new adventures. "But what will we do with all the fish we are going to catch?"

"Well," Peter smiled the smile of the fox. "We'll eat a few, store the rest, wait till there is a shortage, then put them on the market at top dollar and turn a big profit."

"Oh!" said the Lord Jesus, who had that puzzled and pained look in his face that Peter had often observed, as if something that had never crossed his mind just made a forced entry. Peter wondered how someone as obviously intelligent as Jesus could be so slow in some matters.

The next morning at dawn the Lord Jesus and St. Peter were down at the shore readying their boat. And it was just as St. Peter had said. When the other fishermen saw Peter, they sidled over. "Going out, Peter?" they asked.

"Yeah," answered Peter, not looking up from the nets.

"Mind if we come along?"

"Why not?" shrugged Peter, pretending to be bothered by them.

When they left, he glared over at the Lord Jesus and said, "See!"

St. Peter's boat led the way. The Lord Jesus was in the prow hanging on tightly for he was deeply afraid of the water. Now St. Peter was a scientist of a fisherman. He tasted the water, scanned the sky, peered down into the lake—and gave the word in a whisper: "Over there."

"Why isn't anyone talking?" asked the Lord Jesus.

"Shhhh!" Peter shook his head.

The boats formed a wide circle around the area that Peter had pointed to. "Let down the nets," Peter's voice crept over the surface of the water.

"Why don't they just toss them in?" asked the Lord Jesus, who had hopes of learning about fishing.

A second shhhh! came from St. Peter.

The fishermen let down their nets and began to pull them in. But something was wrong. The muscles of their arms did not tighten under the weight of fish. The nets rose quickly; the arms of the men were slack. All they caught was water.

The fisherman rowed their boats over to St. Peter. They were a chorus of anger. "The greatest fisherman in all of Galilee, my grandmother's bald head. You brought us all the way out here for nothing. We have wasted the best hours of the day and have not one fish to show for it. Stick to preaching, Peter." And they rowed toward shore, shouting curses over their shoulders.

The Lord Jesus said nothing. St. Peter checked the nets. He put on a second parade, tasting the sea, scanning the sky, peering into the depths. At long last he looked at the Lord Jesus and said, "Over there!"

No sooner had he said, "Over there!" than the Lord Jesus was at the oars, rowing mightily, the muscles of his back straining with each pull.

And all day long under the searing sun the Lord Jesus and St. Peter rowed from place to place on the sea of Galilee. And all day long under the searing sun the Lord Jesus and St. Peter let down their nets. And all day long under the searing sun the Lord Jesus and St. Peter hauled in their nets. And all day long under the searing sun the Lord Jesus and St. Peter caught nothing.

Evening fell and an exhausted St. Peter raised the sail to make for shore. The weary Lord Jesus held on tightly in the prow. It was then, as the boat glided toward the shore, that it happened. All the fish in the sea of Galilee came to the surface. They leapt on one side of the boat and they leapt on the other side of the boat. They leapt behind the boat and they leapt in front of the boat. They formed a cordon around the boat, escorting it toward shore in full fanfare. Then in a mass suicide of fish, they began to leap into the boat. They landed in the lap of the laughing Lord Jesus. They smacked the astonished St. Peter in the face. When the boat arrived at shore, it was brimming, creaking, sinking under the weight of fish.

It was then, as the boat glided toward the shore, that it happened. All the fish in the sea of Galilee came to the surface.

All the other fishermen were waiting. They gathered around Peter and slapped him on the back. "Peter, you scoundrel. You knew where the fish were all the time and never let on." They hit him on the shoulder. "Peter, you rogue, you put us on. You surely are the greatest fisherman in all of Galilee."

But St. Peter was uncharacteristically silent. He only said, "Give the fish to everyone. Tonight, no home in this village will go without food." After that, he said nothing.

But later, at the tavern with bread and wine between them, Peter looked across the table at Jesus and said, "Go away from me. You go away from me. I wanted the fish to be over them not with them. I wanted the fish to rule them not feed them. You go away from me. I am a sinful man."

But Jesus smiled, not the smile of the fox but the smile that swept over the waters at the dawn of time, the smile that moves the sun and the stars. And he had no intention of going away. There were other fish to catch.

The Higher Math of Sr. Imelda

"Whoever welcomes a prophet
will receive a prophet's reward."
—*Matthew 10:41*

Sister Imelda is a retired member of the Adorers of the Infant Jesus. She helps out in the library of an all-boys Catholic high school. She is the subject of tales, both true and tall.

Once there was a psychologist who came into the classroom of the senior boys to conduct workshops on "values clarification." One of his exercises was to seat two boys across from each other. On the table between them were two lines of coins. One line contained a quarter and a nickel; the other line had three dimes and quarter. The setup looked like this:

Line One	Line Two
quarter	three dimes
nickel	quarter

The rules were simple. One boy (chosen by lot) got to choose one of the lines. If he chose line one, he got to keep the quarter and the other boy received the nickel. If the chooser picked line two, he kept the three dimes and the other boy got the quarter. The chooser could choose either line of coins, but his counterpart had to take the lower amount in that line.

Seven out of ten of the choosers chose line one.

The psychologist pointed out that this was a somewhat surprising result. Had the choosers taken line two, they would have each received thirty cents—five cents more than if they chose line one. But they would have been only five cents ahead of their rivals across the table. When they chose line one, they had five cents less but were twenty cents ahead of their partners. The psychologist concluded that the boys were not motivated by greed as much as by competition. What they wanted more than money was to be as far ahead of the next guy as possible.

What they wanted more than money was to be as far ahead of the next guy as possible.

"Huh, wow! That makes you think," said one of the boys, speaking for all. He said it as if it was a new experience.

Just then, Sister Imelda came into the room with a handful of overdue book notices, each containing a fine.

Now, it is the nature of human beings that the moment we learn something new—especially if it has the potential of tricking another human being—we have to give it a try.

"S'ter, S'ter, come here a minute," called Jimmie Ivoniak. "Sit right down here, S'ter. See the two lines of coins. You get to choose. Take the quarter and I get the nickel. Take the three dimes and I get the quarter. Which one do you pick, S'ter?"

Sister Imelda contemplated the coins for a moment, arched her right eyebrow, and said, "Why don't the two of us take line two together, Mr. Ivoniak? Then we'll have fifty-five cents between us."

For the first time in his young life, Jimmie Ivoniak had nothing to say.

Sister Imelda stood. The boys who had gathered around her divided like the Red Sea as she swept towards the door. Then she stopped, turned, and said, "Even the entire fifty-five cents, Mr. Ivoniak, would not be enough to cover your book fine."

Thus did Sister Imelda clarify the values of the senior class.

"How Come I Felt So Bad?"

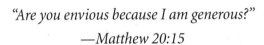

"Are you envious because I am generous?"
—*Matthew 20:15*

You never know what questions kids are going to ask, especially when you are putting them down for the night. That is when there is enough of a slowdown for them to review the day and pursue what is really on their minds.

As Tom tucked in little Tommy, he felt that tonight his eight-year-old son might want to relive the happy events of the day. Tommy's team had won the little league championship that morning. Tommy had three hits and his friend Phil had hit the game-winning home run.

"Pretty good day," Tom said to Tommy as he sat on the side of his son's bed. But Tommy did not respond. The boy looked pensive.

"Dad, you know when Phil hit the homer and everyone ran onto the field and we jumped up and down?"

"Yeah," said the father, not know where this was going.

"I was happy, but inside I felt sort of bad too. How come I felt so bad when Phil got the winning hit?"

Tom wished that his son had asked him about sex. It would have been easier.

The Kaleidoscope

The wind blows where it will.

—John 3:8

The Christmas tree was a gangly forest fir that had no shape. Branches at the top were long and knobby. One stuck out like E.T.'s finger. At the middle was a waistband of short branches, giving the impression the tree was sucking in its stomach for a Christmas photo. Near the bottom, a branch grew straight down. There were ornaments, tinsel, lights and garlands doing what they could, but no amount of cosmetics could camouflage the gaps or cover the bare stretches. The tree's only virtue was that it was tall, but even that worked against it. Its height left so little room for the angel at the top that her wings were bent against the ceiling. On the whole, it was an over-dressed, underdeveloped fir trying unsuccessfully to pass as a Christmas tree.

When my brother Alex saw it, he took a slow sip of his martini and said, "Now I know why they invented artificial trees."

But the presents were stacked beneath it, and we were gathered around it—all my extended family, come from far and near on Christmas Eve (to grandmother's house no less). Each of us was decoratively decked out, but not without a bent wing here or a bare stretch of branch there. The tree was no stranger to our gathering. It fit in. It was one of us. And I like to think it was redeemed by the company it kept.

However, lately I have not been much company. Some sadness has moved into my heart, like a fog that comes off the sea. You do not notice it until it has engulfed you. It's nothing physical. The doctor looked at blood profiles and x-rays and just shrugged. But I am numb. I cannot muster even a passing pleasure. If you slapped my soul, it wouldn't move. Malaise is the word, I guess, but I don't care enough to look it up.

Some sadness has moved into my heart, like a fog that comes off the sea. You do not notice it until it has engulfed you.

I saw my condition clearly last week. My wife Eleanor and I went to a party at some friends of ours who live in a condominium. We parked in the basement and, as we were waiting for the elevator, there was a sudden noise coming from the storage area. I turned and a clothes rack—one of those carts on wheels that people use to transport cleaning and clothes—was coming toward us, splashing through the puddles left by the snow that had melted off the cars. At the front of the rack was a girl of about ten, hanging on to the vertical pole, leaning forward. She reminded me of Kate Winslet leaning over the front of the Titanic. Someone quite long in the tooth played the Leonardo DiCaprio role. I suspect it was her grandfather. He was pushing the rack from behind and had it going fast enough to lift the long, blondish-brown hair of his grand-daughter ever so slightly off her shoulders. Both of them were laughing.

As they sped by, I waved. Then I turned and watched them move down the parking garage until they turned the corner and disappeared. I couldn't get enough of them. As the elevator took us up to the party, I said to myself, "God, I wish I could push that clothes rack."

Eleanor looked at me and said, "What?"

"Nothing," I said. "Nothing, just thinking out loud."

The elevator door opened. The distraction of the party was only a few feet away.

So the scrawny tree was no stranger to my spirit as we

all gathered around it, squeezed into the living room, even overflowing into the dining room. It was time to open the presents. We waited as the patriarchs and matriarchs settled into chairs or claimed a section of sofa. The rest of us either stood or found a piece of floor. I plopped down at the back of the room and leaned against the wall. It was a good spot. I could see most of my family and relatives, but they could not see me. I would be able to catch their expressions as they pulled the hidden treasure from the plundered boxes, but I wouldn't have to pretend I was enthusiastic myself.

Without fanfare, the gift giving began. Presents came out from under the tree and were passed along to their rightful recipient. For an hour the room was filled with the sound of tearing paper and laughing, the sound of tearing paper and "ooing," the sound of tearing paper and kissing, the sound of tearing paper and "ahhing," the sound of tearing paper and thanking. Finally, with the floor a bright, undulating sea of torn wrapping paper, a collective exhaustion set in and we sat for a second of silence amid shambles of Christmas giving.

Then my nephew, who had been playing Santa Claus and handing out the presents with great precision, announced, "The last present goes to Uncle Paul."

I saw it coming toward me, a moderate-sized box with an immoderate bow, being passed along a chain of people from the hand of my nephew to the hand of my grandfather to the hand of my mother to the hand of my sister to the hand of my wife to the hand of my daughter and finally to my own hand. The last present, fingerprinted by the people I love, was in my lap...and I couldn't care less.

I would be able to catch their expressions as they pulled the hidden treasure from the plundered boxes, but I wouldn't have to pretend I was enthusiastic myself.

I looked for a card or name tag, but I could not find one. Then I looked up and saw that everyone's face was turned toward me in Christmas anticipation. I felt a flush of panic that I was going to be found out, discovered in my secret sadness I could not even name.

I quickly ripped the paper, but got no joy from the sound or feel. Underneath was a naked rectangular box that gave no indication of what was inside. I pulled open the top and felt a slight swoosh of air. Inside was a velvet bag with a gold cord knotting the top. I untied the cord and the velvet bag slid down.

It was a large kaleidoscope. The casing was real wood, a dark stained oak that gave it a polished, handsome look. It came with a stand that made a clear statement: "I am not an ordinary, budget-bin kaleidoscope. I belong in a prominent place, displayed on a table or shelf. I do not deserve the back of the closet and, under no circumstances, should I disappear beneath the bed." This was a gift that took itself seriously.

There wasn't a card in the box either. It was a gift without a giver.

"Who do I have to thank for this?" I asked.

Nobody said anything. Finally, my wife said, "Santa, of course!"

It was as if that word, "Santa," was a signal. People got up immediately and were stirring around—asking about dinner or making themselves another drink. The gift giving was officially over, and I was left alone with my anonymous gift.

My wife came over and, holding her dress down with one hand, sat next to me on the floor. Then she said with infinite gentleness and a touch of wickedness, "Aren't you going to look through the kaleidoscope, Scrooge?"

I laughed despite myself and put it to my eye, monocle fit, and turned it. The technicolor pieces twisted and tumbled into a pattern. It was stunning. I turned it again and the pieces fell into chaos and then stepped festively into a new beauty. I took my time as my eye drank in its pleasure. Then I turned it again. I could not get enough of it.

In my ear, whispering, was the voice of my wife: "It was the closest I could find to a clothes rack."

I put down the kaleidoscope and looked at her. I slid my hand under her hair, resting it on the nape of her neck. Then I flicked my hand and her hair lifted off her shoulders, like a little girl's. It was as if some sudden Christmas wind had rushed through the room, bestowing life on those who needed it.

The Kid with No Light in His Eyes

"*The Son of Man came to seek and save the lost.*"
—*Luke 19:10*

A hundred years ago in the summer of 1961 when I was twenty, I was going to be rich. The source of my wealth was going to be a construction job which paid the smacking sum of $3.25 an hour. With this accumulated summer wealth, I was going to roll fat and sassy through the upcoming school year.

The job fell through, and I was forced to do what I had done for five previous summers: be a camp counselor. Of all the undoubted joys of camp counseling, money is not one of them.

It was late in the season when I applied, with the help of the seminary, to be head counselor at a camp connected with a Catholic boarding school. This school took only those kids who had attended the summer camp. The reason for this was not disguised. The summer camp was staffed by eight nuns and four counselors. Part of the task was to observe the kids and sort out the saints from the sinners. The theory was that the best way to spot sociopaths is to watch them play baseball.

When I talked to the head sister, she was delighted. Not only did I have five summers of counseling experience, but in the fall I would start studying theology. She said it was the happiest day of her life. Before the summer was over, she was to regret that remark.

No camp season really starts until there has been a disaster. The campers arrived on Sunday night. On Monday morning someone was missing his hunting knife. By afternoon a baseball glove was nowhere to be found. By canteen time at nine, one of the campers reported losing $5. And you did not have to have "light years" of experience to know we had a thief.

No camp season really starts until there has been a disaster.

It is difficult to know what makes kids eleven and twelve years old steal, especially if they do not really need what they are stealing. But one thing is for sure: they are really bad at it. So, by Tuesday afternoon, we had the culprit. Since I was the head counselor, I sat down with him.

"Why did you do it?" I asked.

"I didn't do it."

"We found the knife and glove in your locker. Why did you do it?"

"I didn't do it."

"Look it," I said, "this is only the second day of camp. We are going to forget this ever happened. No one knows you took the stuff. I am going to return the knife and glove—we are going to forget about the $5—and start over. We are going to wipe the slate clean and begin again."

"I didn't do it."

This kid was not afraid of me in the least. And all the time I talked to him there was absolutely no expression on his face. There was no light in this kid's eyes at all.

On Wednesday afternoon in a rowboat he stuck a fishhook in another kid's leg. And there we were again—me and the kid with no light in his eyes.

"Why did you do it?"

"I didn't do it."

"Stay here," I said. And I went to see the head sister, the one who was so happy to have me.

"Sister," I broke out, "we have a real problem on our hands."

"Before you tell me about it, Mr. Shea," (she was very formal), "I have a few problems I would like to discuss with you. About the record?"

"O yes, the record," I smiled. For you see I had been at many camps but this was the most Catholic camp of them all. Lights went out every night at ten o'clock, and to waft the little darlings into dreamland, they played Schubert's "Ave Maria" over the loud speaker. I thought this was a bit much. So on the second night of camp I substituted a popular camp parody of the time by Alan Sherman: "Hello Mother! Hello Father! Here I am at Camp Granada."

The head sister wanted to know if perhaps I had acted rashly and introduced radical innovations into the life of the camp before I had sufficiently understood its spirit. I said that this was a possibility and that from now on I would consult with her. (This was good training for dealing with bishops.)

"But," I forged on, "we have a real problem. This kid is a flaming sociopath." I had not studied Mark Hart's *Five Words A Day To A Better Vocabulary* for nothing.

"Also about the keys." The head sister was still in control.

"O yes, the keys," I smiled. For you see the head sister kept the keys to the truck and the car on her person at all times. And if you wanted to go anywhere you had to find her and beg for the keys. And she would say, "I hope this isn't for beer, Mr. Shea." And then I would have to lie. Well on the second day of camp I wanted the keys. The sisters lived in a semi-cloistered area above the refectory which had an old rickety staircase leading up to it. I stood at the bottom of the stairs and yelled up, "Sister I need the keys."

"I'll be right down, Mr. Shea."

"That's okay, Sister. I'll come up and get them."

"Don't come up here, Mr. Shea."

"I'm coming, Sister."

And then I stood at the bottom of the stairs and pounded my feet, producing the effect of climbing the stairs.

"Mr. Shea, don't you dare come up here."

And then she arrived at the top of the stairs, habit somewhat askew and car keys in hand. She saw that I had not moved from the bottom step and she glowered.

"You're a very cruel young man, Mr. Shea, a very cruel young man."

I apologized for baiting her with the keys.

"But, Sister," I finally got in, "we have a kid who steals stuff and hurts kids. We have to get rid of him. If the other kids don't kill him, I'm going to."

She said that it was impossible to send him home. His parents had dropped him off and then taken off for vacation. They were going to return in two weeks to pick him up. She had the telephone number of an aunt in case of emergency, but she would not feel right in sending the kid home to the aunt.

"So," she concluded, "we'll have to give him to Sister Ruth Ann."

"Sister Fix-it?" I asked. For this is what the kids called Sister Ruth Ann. She was a retired nun whose only concession to old age and arthritis was a pair of red gym shoes which peeked out from under her habit as she shuffled along. Her father had been a janitor, the rumor mill had it, and she could repair anything, and that was what she did. She went around the camp, painting, planting, and plumbing.

I did not think it was a good idea to give the kid with no light in his eyes to the old nun, but I had just lost twice, so I said okay.

The next morning at seven, Sister Fix-it shook me awake. "Which one?"

"Top of the last bunk."

She walked down to the end of the cabin. I could hear her say, "Wake up. Come. I need you."

Then it started. We would be playing baseball, and you would look up, and out past centerfield would be the old nun and the kid planting something in the earth. We would be swimming, and you would look over and see the old nun and the kid painting the side of the chapel. We would be in eating, and you would look out on the pier and there would be the old nun and the kid

Wherever you saw the old nun, you saw the kid, and wherever you saw the kid, you saw the old nun.

having lunch—two baloney sandwiches and two Orange Crush. Wherever you saw the old nun, you saw the kid, and wherever you saw the kid, you saw the old nun.

The two weeks passed and the parents returned. They parked their car at the back and were walking up to the refectory where the head sister saw everybody. The head sister suddenly appeared on the porch of the refectory and saw me sitting on the hill watching the parents.

"Mr. Shea, come down here."

"Yes, Sister."

All four of us—two parents, one head sister, and one counselor—sat down together. The parents asked what parents have asked since the dawn of time.

"How is our son doing?"

The head sister launched in.

"You lied to us. You told us this boy was doing all right. He is not doing all right. He has stolen other boys' property and viciously hurt one boy. Your son is very troubled."

The mother began to cry, and the father began to plead. "We know. He has been arrested for stealing, and he has been put back a grade in school. But we thought if we could get him into the academy, he might straighten out."

"Well," said the head sister, "it is Sister Ruth Ann's opinion that we should keep the boy here another two weeks." She looked over at me and smiled, and in one "fell swoop" got me back for both the record and the keys. "But," she went on, "he will not be playing with the other campers. He will be working around the camp with Sister. Nevertheless, you will pay as if he were one of the campers."

"Anything," the father sighed.

Now this was a "clean cup" camp. Two weeks of campers were dumped, and another whole new batch brought in. The new ones didn't know the history of the kid with no light in his eyes. They asked me, "Who is the kid who hangs around with the old nun with the gym shoes? Think he wants to play baseball?"

"Ask him."

They asked him. He looked at the old nun. She said, "You go play at baseball, and when you are done, you come back here and we will hoe in the garden."

We would be going out to go horseback riding. The old nun and the kid would be "reconstructing the ark" which was at the entrance of the camp. The kids would yell from the back of the truck, "Wanna go horseback riding?" He would look at the nun. She would say, "You go play at horseback riding, and when you are done, you come back here and we will paint the bench down by the lake."

We would be having swimming races, and he would be standing there watching with those lightless eyes, "Wanna swim?" He'd look at the old nun. "You go now and play at swimming, and when you are done, you come back here. We have much to do."

And so it went for the second two weeks. She let him out, and she reeled him in; she let him out, and she reeled him in. And at the end of two weeks, the kid was integrated into the life of the camp.

His parents came for the second time, and they parked in the back and made their way toward the refectory. I watched them from the hill. The head sister didn't call me in, so I don't know what happened. After about a half an hour, the parents came out and went back and waited by the side of their car.

I think I saw them at the same time the parents did: The old nun with gym shoes and the kid with no light in his eyes were coming up the path that led down to the lake. Even at twelve, he was taller than she was. She had her arm around his waist and a glow on her face like a woman who had found a coin she had long looked for, and with each step, she pulled him against her. She was hip-hugging him as they walked toward his waiting parents. And he let her do it.

"Let Them Be Who They Will Be"

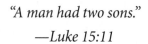

"A man had two sons."
—*Luke 15:11*

hen Jesus said, "There was a man who had two sons. The younger of them said to his father, 'Father, give me the share of the property that will belong to me.' So he divided his property between them."

The Younger Son
On beef,
the meat around the bone is best
On woman,
though, I prefer the plump parts,

What a feast my father throws!
O belly, we're back!
No more watch and rumble
while the swine swill and snort
and I bite through my lip and drool
for a munch on one of the carob pods.
But a love slap on the unclean rumps!
They made me remember my own trough—
DADDY

I rehearsed a speech,
a mumble masterpiece.
With a mouth turned down,
an eyeful of mist,
repentant as a whore with clap:
I whimper:
"Father, I have sinned against heaven
and against thee." (voice falters)
    (Daddy, your little boy has done wrong
    and he's so sorry that he'll never do it again.
    Really, he won't.)
"Do not take me back as a Son:
take me back as a hired hand."
    (But TAKE ME BACK,
    my belly and I do beg,
    you large-lardered,
    stuffed-saddledbagged,
    wine-drenched
    old Daddy.)

Grovel a little to guzzle a lot:
crawl on your belly to feed it.

That is my philosophy.

But the old man upstaged me.
He fell upon me in mid-sentence
ruining my clever act.
But the script was magic.
A robe, ring, and sandals
suddenly appeared;
and this feast fell from heaven.
It was like I was,
what can I say,
a long lost son,
a dead man come back to life.

But I suspect Father is up to something.
No one can be that happy
to see the return of an appetite
that swallowed half an inheritance.
But, then again, I always was his favorite
and I could make him dance to any tune I piped.
Gushy old men are my specialty.
Anyway, the calf is succulent.

I have what I want,
and that is what I have always wanted.

The Older Brother
All these years!
Even the servant boy sensed it.
He would not look at me
as he told me the news:
"Your brother is home,
and your father has killed the fatted calf
because he has him back safe and sound."
He has had ME home—
all these years—
and no music ever greeted ME
as I dragged in
from our fields.
All those mornings!
With him coughing up his night phlegm
and complaining of the cold,
and me throwing a blanket around his bones,
and sitting him on a bench in the sun.
All those days!

With him staring off in the opposite direction
of wherever I was,
growing weary from watching
for the one who does not come,
and me looking up from the earth
to find his back blocking the sky.
All those harvests!
With me, giddy as a child who had found a coin,
yelling for him to come
see the hundredfold crop and sagging vines,
and him coughing and sighing
like the wheat was dust and the grapes were rocks.
All those nights!
With him droning a prayer
and nodding over his food,
and forgetting to bless me before bed.
And me watching for the embrace
he was saving,
hoping for the words
he was hoarding,
eager for an unfeigned arm
around my shoulder,

for a kiss strong enough
to bring blood to my cheek.

Now he tells me that
all these years
we have been
together and have become
one.
"You have been with me always;
and all I have is yours."
I need more, Father,
I need you to run to ME
out of breath and heart-bursting,
not as you are now
with your sensible "Now see here" logic
about the fittingness of feasting
for someone else

All these years!

The Father

I have two sons,
neither of whom wants ME for a father.
So they make me into the father they want.

One makes me into a pimp for his belly.
He thinks he tricks me into concessions,
cons a calf from a sentimental old fool.
He credits my dancing to his piping:
but the music I hear has another source.

He is always empty
so my fullness is hidden from him.
His cunning gives him no rest
so my peace eludes him.
He secretly seizes in the night
what I freely offer in the day.
He wants a father he can steal from.
Instead he has me,
a vine with more wine
than he can drink.
It is hard for him to forgive me

for providing more than he can plunder.
I am abundance.
He must learn to live with it.

The other one counts my kisses.
He wants me to count his.
"For two days ploughing,
take this hug.
For a plentiful harvest,
receive this blessing."
He is so unsure of himself,
he cannot share my assurance.
He lives by measuring what he does not have.
An eye anywhere else
is an eye lost to him.
He thinks I take him for granted;
but I lean on him like a staff.
He is the privileged companion
of my morning pain and evening praise.
I would allow no one else to see
the stumble of my memory,
the embarrassment of my body.

But he credits my love to his loyalty.
He wants a father, indentured to him,
paying him back in affection
for his back-breaking labor.
Instead he has me,
an ancient tree with its own soil.
He does not understand
that he cannot calm his panic with a bargain.
There will be chain between us.
I freely tie my wrist to his.

I have two sons.
Wherever they are,
I go to meet them.
I am their father.
But I am who I am.
Let them be
who they will be.

Lord Love a Duck

"Man, if you know what you are doing, you are blessed.
But if you do not know what you are doing, you are cursed."
—*Codex D of the Gospel of Luke 6:5*

From April to October, every evening at five, the ducks arrived. By seven they were gone.

"Here come the ducks," Tom, who lived on the third floor center section of the condominium, would announce every evening.

"They are Canadian geese, dear." His wife, Marge, corrected him every evening.

"Just in time for cocktails," Tom would respond, rubbing his hands together.

The ducks could be seen at a distance in the sky. They looked as if they were coming in on the clouds. They flew in perfect, squadron formation and landed in "the drink" with honks and hoots, congratulating one another on their successful arrival.

"The drink" was the body of water which was the centerpiece of the condominium complex. It was too little to be called a lake and too large to be called a pond, so the people called it "the drink." Three buildings of seven floors each surrounded "the drink." They cupped it like a pair of hands. Willows wept along the bank.

Each apartment in the three buildings had a balcony which overlooked "the drink." And most of the people gathered on their balconies around five to have a pre-dinner cocktail and greet their evening visitors from the sky.

The ducks were everybody's guests.

Once the ducks had landed, they paddled about in different directions like tourists who had just gotten off a bus. On the land they waddled this way and that, their rear ends doing Mae West imitations.

Once the ducks had landed, they paddled about in different directions like tourists who had just gotten off a bus.

Their presence kept the conversation going. "You should never give a duck a bath," Janice, in six center, shouted over to Alice in six right. "The soap ruins the oil in their feathers, and when they land in the water, they sink and drown."

Phyllis, in five center, overhead this and said to her husband, "Can ducks drown?"

"Why don't you go grab one by the neck, Phyllis, and jam its head under the water and see?" Fred replied without taking his eyes from the evening news on the T.V.

The people fed the ducks bread. They would throw chunks from their balconies onto the ground. The ducks would scurry, their necks stretched out low to the ground, and gobble the gifts. Their whole bodies would shake as the bread slid down their tunnel necks.

"Do ducks have stomachs?" Phyllis asked.

"How do you think they shit?" Fred countered.

"Cows have two stomachs," Phyllis stated.

Fred gave her a stern look before returning to Dan Rather.

Then one evening the scene changed. One of the ducks was limping.

"Look! One's hurt," exclaimed Marge from two center.

This got George Wilbur, in six right, off his chair. He leaned over the railing and watched the duck hobbling along.

"He doesn't seem to be in pain," said a female voice from three left.

"Do ducks cry?" asked Phyllis.

"I have to go to the bathroom," said Fred.

"Throw the bread near the gimpy duck," commanded

George Wilbur, who was a take-charge guy.

The condominium dwellers obeyed. They threw bread directly in front of the limping duck but, hurry as he might, he could not beat the other ducks to it. He went breadless, night after night.

The people were outraged. The gluttony of the other ducks disgusted them. They all agreed that this was the animal kingdom at its worst.

"Here come those selfish ducks," Tom would announce every evening around five.

"Selfish Canadian geese, dear," Marge would correct him.

"Just in time for cocktails." Tom would rub his hands.

On Thursday, after a full week of watching the gimpy duck go without bread, George Wilbur decided to skip his cocktail. Phyllis saw him first.

"Does George Wilbur know what he's doing?"

"George Wilbur never knows what he is doing," said Fred.

"Look at him."

George Wilbur was hiding among the hanging branches of one of the weeping willows. He was wearing a pair of winter gloves and he had a large net in both hands. He looked like a fowler who had escaped from an Old Testament psalm.

When the ducks landed on the water, the entire building leaned over their balcony railings and watched in silence. Once on land the ducks began their mindless, bobbing stroll. The gimp made his appearance.

George's first toss missed. The ducks honked and ran and flew. On his second toss the net floated perfectly through the air and snared the limping duck.

He looked like a fowler who had escaped from an Old Testament psalm.

"Got you, you son of a bitch." George carefully scooped him up from behind. The duck went peaceably.

"I'm taking him to the vet," he yelled up at the spectators.

One and all, they applauded.

They kept him in the utility room in six center overnight. The woman came in with bread soaked in milk. The gimpy duck guzzled greedily.

"Do ducks get fat, like, you know, overweight?" Phyllis asked.

No one answered.

In the morning George put on his winter gloves, placed the duck in a large cardboard box with air holes poked in it, loaded the box into the back of his station wagon, and went to the vet.

George sat in the waiting room, proud that he cared enough to do something.

After a half-hour the veterinarian returned. "You're right. This duck has a very bad leg. The cartilage is rotting away. Some damn fools have been feeding him too much white bread."

Making a Home for Spirit

"He returned to Nazareth
and was obedient to his parents...."
—Luke 2:51

J oseph was worried. He was sick, and he could not count on a conscious death bed to tell his son the only thing he knew that was worthwhile. So while they worked their carpentry trade together, he babbled on, every so often looking up from his cutting and shaving to see if the boy was paying attention.

"Remember, Jesus, whatever we're making, along with it we're always making a home for Spirit. Your mother thinks a home for Spirit is like an empty cup. But I favor a spacious room with a large window for sun—and a door that is hard to find.

"The best way to begin is to clear a space, and the best way to clear a space is stop the mind from judging. Whenever things seem simple and obvious and the mind is feasting on its certainty and outrage, go slow. There is more than you think, only it hasn't appeared yet. Judgment stops the appearance of more. It cuts down people and situations to the little you know. It closes possibilities.

"Also when you do not judge, you often avoid disgracing another. The law is our measure. It is a tool of judgment, but someone always wields it. Do not use it as a hammer to hit or a saw to cut. Our tools are to fashion a table, not to brutalize the wood. The law is a tool to fashion a people of love, but it can break people and lose its sense of purpose. It always fears life will get out of control. So it wants to make examples of people who break it. It feeds and grows strong on transgression. It smacks its lips over scandal. But scandal is not the same as real offense. Scandal can be the irruption of God's love that our feeble minds have yet to understand. So find a way to honor the law and honor the person who, in our limited understanding, has broken it. This is not easy.

Law always fears life will get out of control. So it wants to make examples of people who break it.

"It requires making law work for love. Love is the sun; law its furthest and often weakest ray. If you hold onto love, you will see how the law can reflect it. If you lose love, law will not substitute for it. It will only be something you use to promote yourself and punish others. When you love the person through the law, you shape the law to the reality that is always more than you know. This gives life a chance to breathe and people a chance to change. And the deepest change will not be in other people, but in yourself. Love takes the beam out of your own eye. It does not focus on the splinters in the eyes of others.

"Once something happened and I was tempted to judge and punish. But I held back and waited, and a deeper door opened—the door that is hard to find. I was lead into a room of sun, a home for Spirit. Your mother and you were there—and a presence of light who talked to my fear. I sensed all distances had been traversed, all separations connected. It was a dream, but it was not sleep. The dream awakened me. It took the beam out of my eye. I saw that making a home for Spirit is an endless adventure—like you growing up, my son.

"So see everything twice, Jesus. See it once with the physical eye and then see it again with the eye of the heart. At first glance, you often see an uneven and unusable piece of wood. You may be about to throw it away. But do not be fooled by surface appearances. Look deeper. On second glance, you may see a lovely arm of a chair hidden in its unaccustomed shape. When you see the loveliness, Jesus, embrace it. Take it into your home. Do not hesitate and do not ask questions. Argue with everything, Jesus, but be obedient to love."

The boy listened.

Martha the Good

"Martha, Martha, you are anxious and upset about many things."
—Luke 10:41

Martha is as good as a butter cookie. The Good Samaritan could take lessons from her. If someone is sick, she is first down the block with a meal and chatter. "If you need anything just let me know." She means it.

But her mothering is never neglected. After dinner with the dishes cleared, she sits with her two daughters at the kitchen table and helps them with their homework. She guides Janet, who is fourteen, through the maze of algebra. Next she listens to Alice, her fifth grader, spell the ever-elusive "b-o-u-q-u-e-t."

When the girls are finished and off in their own room, she joins her husband before the television set. "They're doing well," she says with a nod.

"They have a good helper," Tom says.

Martha's husband, Tom, is proud of her. He basks in her goodness. She likes it when she can feel him feeling good about her. It gives her the support she needs to go on.

Martha is also socially concerned. She deplores media hype, government lies, big business ploys. She cannot understand the cruelty and apathy everyone seems to take for granted. At the center of it all (she tells whoever will listen) is rampant self-interest.

"No one cares for anyone but themselves," she says, mounting her soapbox.

"Martha to the rescue," chides Tom.

"Well, they don't," she insists, calming down a bit. She is determined she will not be that way.

Her parish staffs a soup kitchen in the downtown district. The name of the kitchen is Nazareth. One night a week Martha and her oldest daughter go down there and prepare sandwiches and soup for whoever comes in off the street. While the street people are eating, Martha and Janet clean the kitchen. When the street people are done and gone, mother and daughter straighten up and head for home. On their "social action" night Tom cooks and has dinner waiting for them. The conversation usually goes the same way.

"How many tonight?" Tom asks.

"About ten," Martha answers.

"It's good work."

"It's little enough."

"It's a lot."

"I feel sorry for them."

"You should."

"I guess so."

One Tuesday night at 11:30 the doorbell rang. "Who could that be at this hour?" Tom said as he got out of bed to answer it.

"Oh my God!" Martha heard Tom say. She put on her robe and went to the door.

It was Tom's father. The last time they had seen him was at the wedding seventeen years ago. He was drunk then too.

The last time they had seen Tom's father was at the wedding seventeen years ago. He was drunk then too.

"Martha, honey," he smiled, and gave her a hug. Liquor had wasted him. When he grinned, all the bones of his face showed.

The first night he slept on the couch. But by the end of the week the den had been turned into a temporary bedroom. He would sleep away the days and prowl the night. Whatever liquor was in the house always disappeared.

It was Alice, the youngest, who said it. "Gee, Mom. We

have our own personal street person."

Martha was not amused. "Tom, how long is he going to stay?" Her voice had an edge to it.

"He's my father. I can't just throw him out," Tom snapped. Then he playfully grabbed and rubbed the back of Martha's neck. "Give me time," he pleaded.

A month passed and Tom had not found the time.

One night at supper, after the girls had left the table, the family street person slurred, "That Janet of yours is really growing into a ripe young woman."

That night in bed Martha said, "He has to go."

"As soon as I can." Tom turned toward the wall.

Two days later they found him on the floor of the den. The ambulance got him to the hospital in time. The heart attack was not fatal.

He had no insurance. Tom and Martha dug into their savings for a two-week hospital stay. When he was released, they rented a hospital bed. The den was rearranged into a permanent sick room. And Martha the Good became a full time nurse to a cranky, unappreciative, foul-mouthed old man.

One afternoon he yelled from his bed, "God-damnit,

Martha, bring me a beer."

In the kitchen Martha stood perfectly still. Her voice was a whispered monotone, but her ears heard what her mouth said. "God, I hope the son-of-a-bitch dies." Her whole heart was in every word.

And it was as if she had caught God in a rare moment when he had nothing to do but listen; and as a reward for her years of goodness, he tickled her father-in-law's heart into thrombosis and left her staring into the coffin with her answered prayer, wondering how she would ever get back into the garden now that she lived so far east of Eden.

The day of the funeral was also Martha's "social action" night.

"Stay home tonight," Tom said.

"I'm going," Martha said. Her teeth were clenched.

She and Janet opened Nazareth and prepared the soup and sandwiches. But she did not clean the kitchen while the street people ate. For some reason she still does not understand, she sat at the table with a bowl of soup.

Tears came with the first taste and did not stop. But she finished the soup like a medicine she had long avoided.

On the way home in the car her daughter asked, "You

O.K., Mom?"

The words came out slow, with audible sighs between them, the result of some interior, labored birth.

"Next week we'll bring flowers for the tables. Maybe your father and sister will come with us. We'll eat at Nazareth."

The Mother of Soda Bread

*"The kingdom of God is like yeast a woman took
and kneaded into three measures of flour
until the whole mass began to rise."*
—Luke 13:20

S arah had to have it. Not just for herself. Her children, neighbors and friends "oohed and aahed" over it; and everyone urged her to find out how to make it before it was too late. Her mother was getting up in years and it would be a shame if it went with her. So she waited for the right moment and spoke with studied casualness.

"Ma, mind if I watch you make the soda bread and take a few notes?"

"Why should I?" said her mother, and slurped her tea loudly.

I'll never break her of that habit, thought Sarah.

The next afternoon Ma gathered on the countertop all the ingredients necessary for her family-and-neighbor-hood-famous soda bread—flour, sugar, raisins, butter, and a host of ancient spice bottles that were hidden in the back of the cabinet. Then with a deep intake of breath like a conductor the second before a symphony, she began.

Sarah took copious notes. Each pinch and dab and sprinkle were scribbled on her yellow pad. Later on, looking over her jottings, she was puzzled by the entry HDE. Then she remembered. That was shorthand for "hit dough with elbow." For the truth was that abbreviations were needed. When Sarah's mother began to make the bread, she seemed to go into a trance. She moved gracefully around the kitchen and her hands were as swift and precise as a concert pianist's. Sarah had all she could do to keep up.

The next day Sarah taped her notes to the cabinet door and began meticulously to follow the instructions. When she came to the part about elbowing the dough, she looked around to make sure she was alone. She felt a little silly, but then delivered the dough a mighty blow. No pro basketball player ever threw a better elbow.

When she came to the part about elbowing the dough, she looked around to make sure she was alone.

That night at dinner she presented the bread with all the anxiety of a bride's first meal. Her family praised the soda bread extravagantly but unanimously agreed that it was not as good as grandma's.

That made Sarah more determined than ever, and sent her back for a second note-taking session.

The next afternoon her mother began her ritual of

baking. Everything was as Sarah had marked it down. She could not see where she had gone wrong.

"Ma, I did everything just as you did, but it didn't turn out the same."

"You forgot the yeast," her mother said.

"You don't use yeast in soda bread," said Sarah.

"You use yeast in everything," instructed her mother.

"I didn't see you use it."

"When I was kneading the dough, I saw all the faces of all the people who would eat it. That yeast entered the dough and made it bread."

"What are you?" said Sarah, laughing. "Some kind of bread mystic?"

Her mother smiled. But she did not deny it.

My Father's Wealth

*"It is your Father's good pleasure
to give you the kingdom."*
—*Luke 12:32*

I was sitting in class on a hot September Saturday afternoon in 1959 when a lightbulb went on in my brain. I was eighteen, and—yes—it was a Saturday and I was in class.

You see, the school I went to was a high school seminary. We seminarians went to class on Saturday and had Thursdays off instead. According to the wisdom of the time, the point of this was to keep us boys separated from the shenanigans—from football games to dating—that were sure to happen on Saturdays. But being boys first and seminarians second, most of us spent most of the Saturday class time scheming about how to get out of class.

When the lightbulb lit, I suddenly saw a clear way out. In my mind, the Saturday doors of the school had just been flung wide open.

The movie *Ben Hur* had just been released and was getting rave reviews. More importantly for my purposes, the Catholic Legion of Decency had not condemned it. I had heard that Christ himself even made a cameo appearance. It was, therefore, perfect for seminarians.

The movie was playing downtown in the evenings, with matinees on Saturdays and Sundays only. There were no matinees scheduled during the week. Why not, you ask? Because there was no one to go to a movie during the week. Most people were working, and their kids were in school.

Ah, I thought, there are 948 boys who are not in school on Thursday afternoons. Perhaps the theater could be persuaded to have a special matinee on one Thursday, and the high school seminarians could all be persuaded to buy tickets and go to it. And I could do the persuading.

But what, you ask, does this have to do with getting out of class on Saturday?

I'll tell you. Every fall, the school had a "mission drive." This was an effort to raise a substantial amount of money to support the efforts of Catholic missionaries in foreign countries. It was a big deal in the seminary, and each classroom competed against the others to raise the most money. The winning classroom received an award.

One Saturday off.

The lightbulb shone in the darkness, and the darkness could not overcome it. I would convince the theater to have a special Thursday matinee showing of *Ben Hur*. I would buy the tickets from the theater for, say, one dollar each and then sell them to all my Thursday-off-with-nothing-to-do fellow students for, say, $1.50 each. With a turnout of 600—not unimaginable if you knew seminaries and seminarians in those days—I could make a profit of $300 for the missions. This would put my class over the top. A free Saturday was in the making.

Now, I have been told that some theologians of the Middle Ages thought part of the bliss of heaven was seeing your enemies in hell. This, I am sure, is poor theology. But certainly part of my motivation in coming up with this plan of genius was knowing that my friends in other classrooms would be in school some Saturday in the near future, while I and my fellow classmates would be out in the "world" that day.

So, I went to the theater that was showing *Ben Hur* and was directed to a very small office with a very big man in it. He oozed over the side of his chair like a melted cheese sandwich. He was smoking a cigar. "What do you want, kid," he snarled. "I ain't hiring."

I told him my plan.

"I ain't Catholic, kid," he said in a decidedly more friendly manner, "but I'll do it." He paused. "Of course, I'll need $600 up front. I gotta have some assurance."

I went back to school and sought out the priest in charge of the mission drive. I told him about my idea and how much it would raise for the mission drive. Then I came to the punch line. "Father, I need $600 up front."

He looked at me for a long while, then he laughed. "I can't do that, Jack. It's too risky," he said.

I was despondent. I went home to talk to my father. Now, my father was a cop. We did not have a lot of money. I told him what I wanted to do and said, "I need $600."

"So do I," he said. But he gave me the money.

I added "wheeler and dealer" to the growing sense of who I was.

My surefire plan proved to be surefire. All the seminarians came to the Thursday showing of *Ben Hur*. My classroom won the mission drive. I paid my father back in six weeks—with no interest, of course. And I added "wheeler and dealer" to the growing sense of who I was.

And on a Saturday in early November that year, I sat

in the bleachers of a high school football game of some non-seminarian friends of mine and practiced being in heaven.

It is now my father's eightieth birthday party in 1992. There are fifteen of us gathered at a restaurant. I am sitting next to my father. He is lifting a drink to his mouth with both hands. The drink is shaking slightly.

He puts the drink back down and looks at me. "Remember the time I lent you the money?" he asks.

We had not talked about that since 1959, but I knew exactly what money he was talking about.

"Yes," I answer, wondering what had brought this on.

"Did you ever think I wouldn't give it to you?" he asks.

"No, Dad," I reply, "I always knew you would give it to me."

"Funny," my father says, "so did I. I always knew I would give it to you."

My Mother's Best Putt

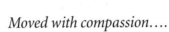

Moved with compassion....
—Matthew 20:34

"Well, we did it," my teacher announced one day in May when I was in eighth grade. "We've finished the work for the year. Now we can have fun."

We still had three weeks of school left, but Sister Rosemary had whipped us through the second semester in record time and we had completed all the assigned material. "Now we can have fun," indeed.

Unfortunately, fun for Sister Rosemary was a never-ending series of spelling bees ("Don't forget to repeat the word before you try to spell it"), geography quizzes ("What is the capital of Nigeria?"), and speed math ("All right, when I say 'go,' turn over the page and solve the problem. The first one finished, raise your hand"). Sister loved intellectual contests of all types—usually with the boys pitted against the girls. Gender wars started early.

I felt all this busy work was really stupid. And I told people so—especially my mother. Those were the days when kids went home for lunch, and as I ate and my mother did things around the kitchen I complained vociferously and daily. My mother was—as usual—firmly on Sister Rosemary's side.

"Why do you think it's stupid?" she would ask.

"Because it is," I'd reply. Did I have to explain the obvious?

"Well, it's only three weeks. Offer it up," she suggested.

Now, "offer it up" was Catholic code for "suffering can't be avoided, so you might as well get something good out of it." Rather than endure meaningless suffering, you could "offer it up"—usually for the "poor souls in purgatory." The idea was that you could gain merits by bearing suffering without complaint and then transfer the benefit to others who needed spiritual help. And nobody needed more help than the poor souls.

However, this redemptive use of my pain did not interest me. I continued my lunchtime assaults on Sister Rosemary.

> *"Offer it up" was Catholic code for "suffering can't be avoided, so you might as well get something good out of it."*

Several times, my mother warned me that she didn't want to hear any more about the matter, but I kept it up.

One day, after a morning of supposedly "fun" quizzes,

I launched a frontal attack on the "stupid" way we were wasting time. I was sitting at the table eating a sandwich, and my mother was washing some dishes. She had her back to me, but I noticed her shoulders suddenly arch and move up around her ears.

I knew I had finally gotten to her! She was now as angry at me as I was at Sister Rosemary. Although I realized I was about to get "blasted," I felt a sense of triumph.

But then my mother's shoulders relaxed. Without turning around, she said, "It'll just take me a minute." She went into her bedroom and came out wearing a sweater. "Down in the basement," she ordered.

I wanted to ask what was going on, but for once in my young life I thought I had best keep my mouth shut.

In the basement, my mother pulled out her golf clubs. "Let's go," she said.

Totally confused, I picked up my own clubs and followed behind her. I was having trouble fathoming what was happening. It looked as if I was skipping school to play golf—with my mother, no less. She was playing the person feared by every Catholic youth of the time: She was being a "bad companion," luring me into wickedness.

We lived only six blocks from Columbus Park, a nine-hole Park District course. It cost a quarter for kids and seventy-five cents for adults to play. As we were walking over to the course, my mother chatted away about this and that, but she did not say one word about school or quizzes or Sister Rosemary or what we were doing. I kept quiet, waiting for a shoe to fall somewhere.

On the fourth hole, my mother was about to putt out. She had about a four-footer. I was holding the flag and waiting. She looked up from the ball and said, "We won't tell anybody about this."

Then she smiled.

Then she made the putt.

Paint the Other Side

"The mustard seed is the smallest of seeds,
but once it is sown upon the earth...."
—Mark 4:31

Claire and Tom were going to be married twenty-five years on Friday. They decided against a party. They had a slew of good reasons. Whom to invite, where to have it, how to be serious about not wanting gifts. Besides, it would cost a fortune.

A week earlier Claire, suspicious that her sister Ann might be cooking up something, phoned her with their decision. "Tom and I will probably just go out to dinner." Then she added the obligatory, "A candlelight dinner." There was silence on the other end. "So no surprises. O.K., Ann?"

More silence. Then, "Caught my thought, did you? Well, O.K. If that's the way you two want it."

From the tone of her voice Claire knew she had surprised her. Ann had not given the anniversary a thought until she mentioned it. She had been the maid of honor, too.

The lone voice for a party was Joyce, their eighteen-year-old daughter. The single reason which she put forward as if it would change everything was, "It only happens once." This observation left Tom and Claire speechless. "Well," Claire finally said, reaching into the storehouse of stock parental responses, "your father and I have already decided."

"Jeez," said Joyce. "You'd think it was a burden."

Claire got sick Thursday night and spent Friday on the sofa in a housecoat with a box of Kleenex. She blew her nose, watched soaps, and pondered.

When Tom got home from work, he took one look at her curled up on the sofa, her nose red, her face without expression. "Psychosomatic?" he ventured.

"Why can't we get worked up for this, Tom? It only happens once."

"Is there something wrong with us?" Tom said to the air between them.

"Not that I know of." Claire pushed her hair back.

"Me neither." Tom plopped into the chair he had plopped into every morning for twenty-five years. "Well, maybe this is just how it is after twenty-five years."

"Oh God," sighed Claire at the prospect of this blah extending indefinitely into the future. It was the first real prayer she had uttered in years.

"Surprise!" Joyce jumped from the hallway. In her hands was a rectangular box wrapped with anniversary paper.

"It looks like a half gallon of booze to me," Tom said.

"Maybe we should stay home and get drunk."

"Wrong!" said Joyce.

Next came an operatic "Happy Anniversary" accompanied by a dance that combined ballet and bugaloo. On the final chord Joyce deposited the box in Claire's lap. The Kleenex was snatched away.

On the final chord Joyce deposited the box in Claire's lap. The Kleenex was snatched away.

Claire opened the card. On the cover was an unshaven man, in T-shirt, baggy pants, and slippers, plopped down in front of the T.V. His right hand held a can of beer which rested on his pot belly. At the other end of the sofa was a woman in curlers, face cream, and housecoat, darning a sock. Her finger stuck through a hole in the sock and she was staring stupidly at it. The inscription read: "To a still handsome man and a still beautiful woman on their silver anniversary."

Claire glared at Joyce.

"Look inside, Mom."

Inside was a picture of a teenage girl, ratty hair, braces, freckles, pimples, jeans with a hole in the knee, and a T-shirt which read, "Puke!" The inscription read: "From your still beautiful daughter."

Claire let out a "short snort," which is what Tom calls "her laugh when she is trying not to." She passed the card to Tom.

"I don't remember posing for this," he said, staring at the pot-bellied man on the front.

"Wrong!" said Joyce. "Open it, Mom."

Claire carefully unwrapped the box and unlatched its notched cardboard top.

"What is this?" she exclaimed as she pulled out the tissue-wrapped object.

"Careful, Mom."

In Claire's hands was a large, Waterford crystal vase. The last light of the day was streaming through the west window. It caught the case and reflected along each cut of the glass. The sun danced on the crystal.

"Oh God, it's beautiful," said Claire softly.

Tom was stunned. He could think of nothing to say so

he said, "Where did you get the money?"

"I robbed a bank."

"What? No flowers?" was his comeback.

Joyce disappeared. Tom reached for the Kleenex.

Joyce was back as quick as she left. In her hands were yellow mums. She put them on the table, ran into the kitchen, filled the gravy pitcher with water, and poured the water in the vase. She arranged the flowers one by one and fluffed them carefully.

"Renoir or Matisse or somebody says you must carefully arrange flowers," Joyce instructed. She put the vase on the table between the sofa where her mother was and the chair her father sat in.

"Then when you are done," she continued, "you turn the flowers around and paint the other side. She turned the vase around so that Tom and Claire both saw the side that was hidden from them. "There," Joyce said.

"Who told you that?" Tom asked.

"My art teacher."

"Smart man that Renoir or Matisse or somebody."

"Come here," said her mother. Claire kissed her. "Thanks, darling. It means more than you know."

"My turn," said Tom. Joyce came over and sat in her father's lap. He kissed her nose like he used to do when she was a little girl. "The last eighteen years were the best of the twenty-five," he said.

"I agree," said Claire.

For a long time they all looked at the vase. There did not seem to be a need to say anything.

Finally, Claire bounced up from the sofa. "Make reservations for three at someplace expensive. I'm going to get dressed."

She walked down the hall to her bedroom; and from the view her husband and daughter had, it looked like her housecoat lifted off the floor with each step.

"Is Mom skipping?" asked Joyce incredulously.

"Your mother always skips," said the man who had been married twenty-five years.

The Phone Call

"While still a long way off, his father saw him...."
—*Luke 15:20*

"Ma, come to the table," Ellen said in a voice that betrayed nothing.

It was Christmas afternoon. The five Dolans—Tom and Ellen, their children Marge, Patrick and Catlin—and Ellen's mother, Marie McKenzie, had gone to church, opened presents, and lingered forever over a Christmas drink. Dinner was now on the table.

Marie said she was not hungry. She rocked back and forth in her favorite chair. On the table next to her was the phone.

"Ma, if she is going to call, she will call. Come to the table."

Marie just rocked.

Ellen gestured her husband Tom into the kitchen. "I spend all day on this meal and she is letting it get cold. This is the thanks I get. All year I take care of her. Take her to bingo, the hair dresser's, church. And every holiday she sulks there waiting for that daughter of hers to call."

Tom had heard all this before. "I don't think she's sulking," said Tom. "I'll take care of it."

Tom went back into the living room, right past Marie at her telephone post, and up the stairs to their bedroom. Marie pretended she didn't see him.

Tom took their phone listings out of the dresser drawer and dialed the California number.

"Yeah!" said a groggy man's voice.

Oh no, thought Tom, not another one. "Is Ann there?"

"Minute."

"Hello."

"Ann, this is Tom. Merry Christmas. Call your mother."

"Tom, for Christ's sake, it's only noon out here, I'll call her later."

"Ann, this is Tom. Merry Christmas. Call your mother."

"Now, Ann. We can't get her to come to the table and eat. Ellen is doing a slow burn."

"So what's new?" She waited, but Tom said nothing.

"O.K. I'll call."

Tom was halfway down the stairs when the phone rang. Marie answered it on the second ring.

"Hi ya, Mom. Ellen feeding you enough?"

"Oh Annie, it's so good to hear your voice."

"Good to hear yours too, Mom. I went to midnight Mass and was sleeping late." She reached under the covers and gave Hank a squeeze. He didn't move. He had fallen back to sleep.

"By the way, Mom, I got your check. Thanks. I needed it."

"You're welcome. When will you be in Chicago?"

"Spring sometime. I'll let you know."

"I miss you."

"You've got Ellen right there, Mom." Her voice got louder as if her mother were hard of hearing.

"Would you like to talk to her?"

There was a moment of silence. "Why not?"

"Here she is."

Ellen had been listening to each word from the kitchen doorway. She walked toward her mother, wiping her hands on her apron. Marie held out the phone. The cord was stretched to the full.

Ellen took the phone. "Merry Christmas."

"Merry Christmas," returned Ann.

Ellen gave the phone back to her mother.

"There," Marie said to anyone who was listening. Her

voice had a sense of accomplishment as if she had just carried a great weight up a forbidding hill and set it down right where it should be. "Merry Christmas," she said out loud to herself.

Then Marie puckered a kiss into the phone's receiver and said, "Bye, Annie, don't let the bedbugs bite."

"Oh, Mom," Ann managed before her mother hung up.

Marie came immediately to the table. The children were stifling laughs; Tom was smiling; Ellen was staring at the plate.

They recited grace together. The food was passed and piled high on each plate.

Marie poured the tea into her cup, poured the tea from the cup onto her saucer, then blew on it to cool it off. A forkful of dressing went into her mouth.

"Delicious," she said with her mouth full.

"Oh, Mom," sighed Ellen.

The Rock

An angel of the Lord rolled back the stone
and sat on it.
—Matthew 28:2

The teacher decided that during the first three days of Holy Week the eighth grade class would put on a passion play. There would be six performances with different grades attending each performance. In this way the eighth graders would learn the passion according to St. Matthew and so would the entire school.

It seemed like a good idea.

As often happens with good ideas, there were a few snags. There were more eighth graders than there were parts in the passion play or the need for stage hands, set designers, etc. So the teacher succumbed to another good idea—to move in the direction of imaginative, avant-garde theater. She cast every animate and inanimate reference in Matthew. She cast:

- the tree from which Judas hanged himself
- the broken vase of perfume
- five people simulating an earthquake
- three people doing a credible job of imitating thirty clattering pieces of silver on the temple floor
- bystanders
- more bystanders
- still more bystanders

She also cast the rock that blocked the entrance to the

tomb of Jesus. This was not a difficult task; it was a matter of typecasting. There was a boy who had, as his mother put it, "sprouted early." He was definitely bigger than a bread box. He was also, bent over with his hands clasping his ankles, a perfect boulder.

"John," the teacher said, "you will be the rock—the one blocking the tomb, not the Apostle Peter. (Teachers cannot avoid puns, especially when they are teaching religion.)

For the Angel of the Lord, who pushes the rock aside, she chose the most petite girl in the class—Tinkerbell one size up. The contrast, the teacher felt, was positively biblical.

The first performance was for the third grade. The play was predictably moving along with the usual sniggers and laughs until the Angel of the Lord appeared. With her little finger outstretched, she nudged the rolled up rock. He somersaulted away from the entrance of the tomb, staying perfectly rolled up. Then the angel sat on him, making the stone of death the throne of the Lord—just as it says in the Gospel of Matthew.

The audience went wild. They cheered and chanted, "Rock! Rock! Rock!" Afterwards they swarmed him for autographs. He modestly signed, "Rock." This happened at performance after performance.

Thus a star was born.

Also a critic. The teacher was not sure all this attention was good for the Rock. Perhaps the glory should be shared. She took the Rock aside and suggested that he play the tree from which Judas hangs himself. Someone else should have a chance at being the rock. The Rock said he did not think this was a good idea. "I like being the rock," he said.

The teacher responded (with what she later thought was the best question of her career), "Why?"

"I like letting Christ out of the tomb," the Rock said.

"But, John, the rock isn't rolled back so Christ can get out. He is already gone." (Teachers are always quick to correct.) "The rock," she pointed out, "is rolled back so that the women can see in."

The Rock's face twisted as he floundered for the first time in the deep waters of the spirit. "Well," he said, "how did he get out if the rock was still stuck in the hole?"

This is the type of question all teachers fear. There is an answer, but it is light years beyond what the questioner is able to handle. The teacher remained silent, searching for words. But the Rock found the words before the teacher did.

"Well," he said, "I guess huge rocks are no big thing for God."

Thus did the Rock roll back the boulder from his own mind and see into the empty darkness of the Easter revelation.

> *"Well," he said,*
> *"I guess huge rocks*
> *are no big thing for God."*

The teacher said in a quiet, choking voice that he should continue in the role of the rock, since he knew the part so well.

"Scaring Ain't So Bad"

"Do not be afraid...."
—Luke 12:4

"It was a long time ago, but I still remember it," said the old man as he closed his eyes to help sharpen his memory.

"It was late in the afternoon. A terrible storm was brewing. The sky was low and dark. I was out in the field. It was no place for a nine-year-old boy to be, so I made for an old shed on the farm where we kept tools and such. But I didn't make it before the storm hit.

"Fierce winds, pelting rains, lightning, thunder—I could barely see. I finally found the shed. Once inside, I crouched in a corner, sitting on some rolled-up rope.

"The shed was old, and the wooden slats had separated. When lightning hit, it sent shafts of light streaking through the cracks. The darkness in the shed would light up and then go dark again. It was like someone was standing in the room and turning a light switch on and off.

"Suddenly the door of the shed swung open. A massive, bearded man in drenched clothes burst inside and shook himself like a dog. Then he saw me, crouched in the corner. He looked back out the open door at the storm and then back at me. He yelled in a loud, deep voice, 'Ah, boy. He's trying to scare us today.'

"Well, that did it. I was already wet, cold and frightened. The last thing I needed was this giant of a strange man bellowing at me. I started to cry.

"The man came and sat down next to me. Then he took his fist—it was the size of a sledge—and slammed it into my shoulder. I could feel his breath on my face. 'Scaring ain't so bad, boy,' he said. Then he laughed."

Shame on Al

*"Do you think these Galileans were
the greatest sinners in Galilee
just because they suffered this?
By no means!"*
—Luke 13:2

Al had died jogging, and his friends knew why.

"You don't start to jog when you're fifty-three," one said.

"I read somewhere that you should start off walking fast and gradually build up to running," said another.

"Let's face it," chimed in a third. "Al's whole lifestyle was heart attack material. He was a compulsive overachiever. He hadn't taken a real vacation in over three years."

"True," the other two said in unison.

Now that they had buried Al with blame, the future opened, endless, before these three pilgrims—if only they were cautious.

Shenanigans at Cana

On the third day,
there was a wedding in Cana of Galilee,
and the mother of Jesus was there.
—John 2:1

The Inspired Imagination

When the wine gave out, the mother of Jesus said to him, "They have no wine." And Jesus said to her, "Woman, what concern is that to you and to me? My hour has not yet come." His mother said to the servants, "Do whatever he tells you" (John 2:3-5).

The Answering Imagination

"Come now, my Son,
do you tease these grey hairs?
Late and laughing you arrive
and find me finding you.
An entreaty is my greeting.
'They have no more wine.'
But you sweep me up
in mock debate,
a young man's arms
around my seriousness,
wresting from me a conspiratorial smile.
'What has that to do with me?'
you say
winking words
which invite the memory of our meals.
And I tell you quick,

in hushes,
how I
lit the fire in your eyes
and held your head of dreams
and poured water in your hands
when you came burning
from the desert sands.
Beyond that,
I say,
you and I
are strangers,
I say.
But games aside
I say,
Jesus,
I say,
These empty glasses
mock your father's feast.
'My hour has not yet come,'
you say,
making me say it all
right here

in the midst of sober guests.
You hold me now
in roles reversed,
son giving birth
a mother young again.
Steward,
I say,
this man who kisses my eyes,
this Son of my love
has need of a canyon
to hold the grapes
that his fast feet
will crush to marriage wine.
Now,
the teeth of our laughter
blinds the steward
who does now know
what we do,
my secret friend.
Your hour is the minute
the wine fails."

The Shoelace

"Mercy…from generation to generation."
—*Luke 1:50*

In a moment of madness, I agreed to do a series of workshops on storytelling in Ireland.

On the sleepless plane ride to Dublin, I pondered the real folly captured by the phrase "bringing coals to Newcastle." What idiocy was I undertaking—telling and talking about stories in the spiritual home of storytelling?

But the people were gracious and forgiving, and the humble truth soon became evident. I was there to learn, not to teach.

On the first day, I sat in a small group as a woman of about seventy-five told a story from her childhood. This is her story, flattened by print and my memory lapses, but impoverished most of all by the absence of her wonderful, soft, lilting voice.

"I was one of fourteen children," she said, "and my mother tried to put order in everything that had to do with our brood. Every Sunday we would walk to the church about three miles away. But before we set out, there was a home ritual every bit as set in its ways as what the priest did at Mass.

"There was only one mirror in the house, and my mother would stand in front of it. Then each of us would queue up and pass between my mother and the mirror. As we did, she would straighten us up and comb our hair. After this combing we could go out and play. When everyone was done we would gather and walk to church.

"One Sunday, I was about third in the queue. My mother looked down the line and saw that my little sister did not have a shoelace in her shoe. My mother looked at me and said, 'Go back and get your sister a shoelace.'

"But I did not want to lose my place, so I didn't budge. When my turn came, I stepped between my mother and the mirror. My mother said nothing. She simply combed my hair and off I went to play.

"I came in a little while later. My little sister—the one without the shoelace—was between my mother and the mirror. My mother bent down and took a shoelace out of her own shoe and put it in the shoe of my little sister. When I saw this, I went into the back of the house and got a shoelace. I came out and knelt at my mother's feet and put the shoelace in her shoe. As I did this and while she was combing the hair of my little sister, she reached down with her free hand and stroked my hair."

The woman stopped telling her story and looked down. The people in the group said nothing until one man asked, "Are you done?"

She nodded. Then the man began to tell one of his stories.

After the session, I was walking around outside when the woman who had told the story walked by. I stopped her and said, "Your story blew me away."

"What?" she asked, and I realized that my "Yankism," as they called them, was causing her bewilderment.

"It was rich and moving," I explained. "I don't know what it means, but I was moved by it."

"It was stupid," she said. "I shouldn't have told it."

"No," I replied. "We are all better for having heard it."

"Thank you," she said, and then she walked on.

While I was conducting the workshops, I would pass the long, civilized Irish afternoon breaks sitting under a tree smoking a cigar. On the fourth day, the woman who had told the story approached me.

"Where is your cigar?" she asked.

"It's in my room," I answered, "but I am too tired to go get it."

"I noticed you didn't have one, so I bought you a cigar," she said. She handed me a cigar.

"Thank you," I said.

I looked down and fiddled with the cellophane wrapper. When I looked up, the woman was gone. As I am smoking the cigar—thinking of nothing in particular—it suddenly dawns on me: the cigar is the shoelace, the cigar is the shoelace.

*"The cigar is the shoelace,
the cigar is the shoelace!"*

During the next session, I saw the woman seated in the back of the room. As soon as I was finished, I pushed through the crowd and found her. I loomed over her and said with way too much enthusiasm, "The cigar is the shoelace, the cigar is the shoelace!"

She looked up at me and stuck out her chin. "I know that," she said. She looked down and then looked back up at me. "It was a pact with my mother," she said with emotion. "It was a pact with my mother."

And as she said this, she hit her heart twice.

Star Gazer

*"You cannot tell by careful watching
when the kingdom of God will come."*
—*Luke 17:20*

Since his daughter was only three and too young to buy him a Father's Day gift, he purchased one for himself.

The telescope was magnificent; it was a Discover Deluxe. It had three lenses building up to two hundred and twenty-seven magnification. It had a counter-balanced equatorial mounting and included a diagonal prism, sun projector screen, and an SLR reflex finder scope. The salesman threw in an accessory tray. Mounted on its tripod next to the window it was aimed like a rifle at the stars.

Every night after dinner the owner pasted his eye to the viewfinder and scanned the heavens for movement, excited over the patterns of light a million miles over his head.

At his feet his daughter played.

Twenty into Fifty Goes a Hundredfold

*"Let the little children come to me,
for to such as these belongs the kingdom."*
—Mark 10:13

ig Jerry groaned when his wife told him he had to go to the store. It was the Wednesday before Thanksgiving and the grocery store would be Grand Central Station. But when he heard that one of the missing ingredients was cranberry sauce, he nodded reluctantly.

"How could you forget the cranberry sauce?" he muttered.

But when his wife yelled from the upstairs bedroom, "Take Little Jerry with you," Big Jerry knew how she could forget the cranberry sauce. This was all part of a bigger plot.

Lately, Big Jerry's wife had been on his case. He wasn't spending enough time with his son. "He needs you, Gerard." Always "Gerard" when there was a lesson to be given. "Just because he's gotten older, that doesn't mean you two have to be so far apart. He's only eleven, you know." Always "you know" when she thought he didn't know. Big Jerry did not like these chiding lectures. It made him feel that he was a bit of a fool; and anyone who had done as well as he had in business was no fool.

Big Jerry stuck his head into the den.

"Want to go to the store?"

Little Jerry buttoned the television dead, and was at

his father's heels.

Big Jerry knew that sometime tomorrow Little Jerry's mother would probe, "What did you and Jerry talk about when you went to the store?" She was hoping for something significant, like the facts of life or the value of a buck.

So Big Jerry tried to get a conversation going.

"How's school?"

"O.K."

"How's your basketball team doing?"

"Lousy."

"What were you watching on T.V.?"

"A movie."

Big Jerry put his foot on the gas. This is normal, he thought to himself, this is normal.

At the store the cranberry sauce, five cans, was scooped up. Big Jerry had feared they might be out of it. They also found the lettuce, nuts, diet Coke, pie crust mix, rolls, orange juice, and something called nutmeg.

When they turned out of the last aisle, they saw the people. The line at the Under Ten checkout counter was over ten people long.

"Grand Central Station," muttered Big Jerry.

"What?" asked Little Jerry.

"Lot of people."

"Yeah."

The checker was a teenage boy and he was carrying on a conversation with the neighboring checker, a teenage girl. It was about a

By the time they got to the front, Big Jerry was steaming. But he said nothing.

party both had been to and both had hated. To Big Jerry's ears every other word was "boring" and "really."

More work and less talk, thought Big Jerry. He noticed the other people in line were giving each other exasperated looks. Big Jerry began to mumble under his breath. He noticed the checker had a bad case of acne.

By the time they got to the front, Big Jerry was steaming. But he said nothing. He just put a fifty dollar bill on the counter.

The checker, happily gabbing away, rang up a $19.35 charge. When Big Jerry saw how much it was, he picked up his fifty and put down a twenty.

The checker did not notice the switch, and gave him $30.65 in change. Big Jerry hesitated. This kid deserves to be taken, he thought. Little Jerry was at his side.

"I gave you a twenty," Big Jerry said.

"No you didn't. You gave me a fifty."

"I gave you a twenty."

"I saw the fifty," the checker insisted.

"Look in the drawer!" Big Jerry's words came out as a growl between clenched teeth.

The checker checked. "Oh yeah." He took all but the sixty-five cents back.

In the parking lot a man came up behind Big Jerry and his son. "You should have taken that jerk for the thirty."

In the car Little Jerry said to his father, "That was neat, Dad." And he began to talk—about school, about basketball, about the movie he was watching on T.V.

Big Jerry tried to listen, but he didn't hear much. For three insights, in rapid succession, raked his mind.

If Little Jerry hadn't been there, he would have grabbed the thirty and walked.

His wife was wrong. Little Jerry didn't need him: he

needed Little Jerry.

And he was glad tomorrow was Thanksgiving.

Waking Up on Christmas Morning

*"You will find a child wrapped in swaddling clothes
and lying in a manger."*
—Luke 2:12

A dam and Eve woke up. They were hungry and thirsty.

Later, on reflection, they did not know if they woke up and were hungry and thirsty, or if hunger and thirst had awakened them.

But they ate and drank, and they were full. It was good.

Six hours later they were hungry and thirsty again.

They said to one another, "We must not have done it right."

So they ate and drank very carefully, savoring every sip and chewing every bite, and they were full. It was good.

Six hours later they were hungry and thirsty again.

So a third time they ate and drank, taking even greater care in chewing and sipping. It was good.

Then it dawned on them. That is the way it was going to be. Hungry and thirsty, then eating and drinking. Then once again, hungry and thirsty, then eating and drinking. Then once again....

It was not enough.

They shouted out their frustration. "What are we? Asses tethered to a feeding trough? Oxen tied to a manger?"

God heard this shout and took their protest as a

prayer. He sent an angel named Gabriel to a town named Nazareth to a virgin named Mary.

Gabriel said, "Adam and Eve hunger and thirst, and you must prepare a feast."

Mary spread herself like linen tablecloth on the earth and the Son of the Most High was born. Shepherds attended his birth and found new flocks to tell what they had seen and heard.

One day they came upon Adam and Eve roaming around outside the garden. The shepherds knew that what they had to say, Adam and Eve wanted to

Adam and Eve were not sure of all that the invitation entailed, but they decided they needed some direction to their roaming.

hear: "We bring you glad tidings of great joy meant for all the people. There has been born to you a child, the Messiah and the Lord. Go to Bethlehem and you will find a child wrapped in swaddling clothes and laid in a manger."

Adam and Eve were not sure of all that the invitation

entailed, but they decided they needed some direction to their roaming. They set out for Bethlehem, the house of Bread. When they arrived at the birth, they were surprised to see an ox and an ass grazing around the manger. As they walked past them, Adam and Eve nodded. Did they know the beasts? Then they looked down at the child wrapped in swaddling clothes and laid in a manger. Before long they knelt.

Mary took the hand of Eve and placed it on the chest of the child, over his heart. The mouth of the child opened and Adam ate from the mouth of the child.

Then Adam and Eve spoke as one: "We tie ourselves to this manger."

Why Bother?

"We had to celebrate and rejoice
because this brother of yours...."
—Luke 15:32

"Why bother?" is what Margaret Mary Mulligan told her husband, Michael Joseph Mulligan, in June of 1948 when, upon his retirement from Sears after thirty years, he proposed they take their granddaughter, who had just graduated from grammar school, and go back to Ireland to see his oldest brother. Margaret, as was her custom, repeated her opinion: "Why bother?"

But when he told his granddaughter, she was delighted and asked, "Gramp, are you and Gram going to go back to live in Ireland?"

"Why should I?" he answered without taking the pipe out of his mouth. "I starved there."

And indeed he had. He was the second son of four sons and three daughters. His older brother was obviously in line for the farm. That was the way it was. There was not much for him and the others to do but move along. And the sooner the better. For what food there was would go farther with one less. So, as he likes to tell it, he threw his shoes over his shoulder to save the wear and tear, walked barefoot over the mountain, and got on the boat for America. That was May 1908.

First, there was a series of jobs in New York—stock

boy, wagon driver, street repairman, a humiliating stint as a servant—"Hey, Paddy, get the dog." Then he took a chance. He moved to Chicago, and with some luck and a good word from a cousin's cousin, he landed a steady job at Sears. He met Margaret and settled down. Three children came along but so did the Great Depression. The little prosperity they had was wiped out.

But with careful planning—scrimping here and saving there—he got back on his feet. Just as he was standing up, he looked around to find out he was old. When it was his wife Margaret's turn to speak at the retirement party, she said, "Ah, Mike, where did it all go? Where did it all go?"

Through the years, Michael Thomas Mulligan kept in touch with his older brother. Every year at Christmas he wrote a letter telling the news he could remember. He was not much of a letter writer, and so his yearly epistles often began, "Not much new here." But he always sent a check. After the first of the year, a return letter would arrive. More often than not it began, "Not much new here either." The check was never mentioned.

But in June 1948, the day after Margaret had said,

"Why bother?" he wrote a letter out of season. "Margaret and I, and our granddaughter, are coming to Ireland for a visit. Would you be home on July 11 in the evening?" A return letter arrived on the last day of June, one day before the train to New York and three days before the sailing to Ireland. It read: "I would. We will be expecting you for dinner."

On July 11, Michael Thomas Mulligan, the second son of four sons and three daughters, rented the newest model Packard he could find, put on his three-piece, broad-lapelled, broad-striped suit, placed his large gold watch in the pocket of his vest and ran the gold chain prominently to the vest pocket, looked approvingly at his wife Margaret in her best hat and dress, and told his granddaughter, "No pedal pushers. I want you to wear a dress." He was on his way to see his older brother.

The stone and thatch cottage was much like he remembered it. Only it seemed father from the main road and by the time they got there the car was covered with mud. It might as well have been a '32 Ford. Gerald John Mulligan and his wife stood at the door. "Jerry," said the younger brother with his hand extended. "Mike," said the older brother taking it. Their eyes never met. Inside the table was already set.

The dinner was plain and good. The talk was general—about the brothers and sisters, America, children, Ireland, the war. The granddaughter escaped to the room where she was to sleep as soon as she could. She propped herself up with a pillow and began reading a Nancy Drew mystery. Not much later the wives, sensing they should, said goodnight. The two brothers sat alone. After some time the older brother broke the silence.

"Are you now a rich yank?"

"I am not," said the younger brother. "Are you now a prosperous land owner?"

"I am not," said the older brother.

The older brother stood up, moved to the cabinet, got a large loaf of fresh bread and a knife, and sat down. The younger brother stood up and went to the back bedroom. Margaret lay on the one bed and his granddaughter, peering into a book, lay on the other. "Is it all right with him?" Margaret asked. "Get some rest," her husband said. He opened the suitcase and rummaged his arm under the neatly-folded clothes. His hand brought out a quart bottle of Kentucky Bourbon. "Is it all right with him?" she said again. "Get some rest," he said. But he smiled, and for the firs time since they arrived in Ireland, she thought she might.

In the kitchen sat the two brothers and between them the bread the older brother had wrested from the stubborn land and the bottle the younger brother had brought back from the far country.

The first up in the morning was the granddaughter. She tiptoed out of the room without waking her grandmother. The kitchen table was filled with crumbs. In the middle of the crumbs were a knife and an empty bottle. The door to the cottage was open. She took it as an invitation and went outside.

The door to the cottage was open. She took it as an invitation and went outside.

The new day had just begun. The sun was climbing into the clear sky. It shimmered off the ocean in the distance and lit the land all the way up to the cottage. In the middle of the field stood the two brothers, pipes in their mouths, inspecting the earth the way a mother checks a newborn baby. "They must have been up all night," the granddaughter thought to herself.

Then the brothers turned, saw her, and waved. And side by side, stride by stride, step by step, they came toward her, and although she herself had never yet stayed up all night to beat back the darkness with her love, she knew that when her time came she would be able to do it. And when they came within earshot, she shouted out to them, "O wow! You made it all the way to morning!"

The Woman and the Kid in Lincoln Park

*"If your brother or sister has something against you,
leave your gift at the altar...."*
—Matthew 28:2

One Saturday morning I was smoking a cigar in Chicago's Lincoln Park and looking over toward the zoo. Ahead of me, turning onto the far end of the walk, was a young woman about the age of thirty-five and a boy of eight or nine.

They were walking toward me down the walk. Grassy hills sloped up on both sides of them. I watched them while I puffed on my cigar. The woman suddenly turned, grabbed the boy's hand, and said something to him. I couldn't hear what she said, but whatever it was pushed his button. He took a swing at her—but it was one of those eight-year-old swings that by the time it gets there has lost everything.

Besides that, the woman ducked under it like a skilled boxer, and as he swung she pulled him against her, his face into her stomach. The boy flailed away at her shoulder blades. Then he tried to kick her. When he tried to kick her he lost his footing and slid down a little bit. But the woman had a tight grip on him and pulled him up. Then she took his hair, pulled his head back, and looked down on him. Even though it was far away, I could see he was crying.

Then she lost her grip. The boy spun away from her and ran up the side of the hill. She began to run after him but, although she was stronger than he was, she was not as fast. He got away from her.

The woman went back to the sidewalk and began to walk again toward me. When the boy got far enough up on the top of the hill, he turned around and yelled, "I don't like you!"

The woman yelled back, "You don't have to like me. You have to listen to me!"

When the boy got far enough up on the top of the hill, he turned around and yelled, "I don't like you!"

It was only then that I was sure she was his mother.

What happened next was like a scene from an old cowboy movie. The mother was the wagon train down in the valley and the son was the Indians up on the hill. He'd come down the hill and get close to her. She'd go after him and he'd run away. This happened about two or three times—he'd come down and get close, then run away; come down and get close, and then run away.

Finally, he got too close and, in the three fastest steps

of her adult life, she tackled him. She threw him down on the ground, sat on his stomach, pinned his arms against the grass with her knees, and then gave him a nuggie on his head.

Exhausted, she rolled off him and lay there on the grass huffing and puffing. (Thirty-five-year-olds can't do a lot without huffing and puffing.)

The boy sat up and just did nothing for a minute. Then suddenly he jumped on her and began to tickle and tickle and tickle and tickle and tickle and tickle her. And she began to laugh and laugh and laugh and laugh and laugh and laugh. Then he began to laugh and laugh and laugh and laugh and laugh and laugh.

Finally there was only the sound of their laughter and the smoke of my cigar rising like incense over Lincoln Park.

The Woman at the Well

Jesus was tired and he sat by the well.

It was noon.

—John 4:6

Those who have ears to hear, hear this story. Those who have eyes to see, see this scene. Anything can happen at a well.

The man who was sitting on the small stone ledge that circled the well slid off, turned to the woman who had just arrived, smiled and said, "I'm thirsty."

She had seen him at a distance. She had stopped to readjust the yoke which straddled her shoulders. A bucket hung from both ends of the yoke, and when her steps were not perfect, and they seldom were, the wood cut into the flesh along the nape of her neck. She took the pain for granted, but from time to time she stopped to shift the weight to more callused skin. From bruise to bruise, she thought, it was as she straightened from her bent posture, to gauge the last ground left before the well, that she saw him. He appeared to be waiting for her.

Her mind raced. She thought of turning around and making for the village. But if he wanted to, he could easily overtake her and take what he wanted. Then, she cursed. Why did she not come earlier in the day with the other women? She knew why. But right now that humiliation looked better than this danger.

Then a plan formed out of her panic. She could see

by his dress that he was a Jew and he would probably walk away. Most likely after some quick insult and with a great show of disdain. If not, she could make him go. She would steel herself, hide her mind, harden her heart. She knew how. She had been there before. It was not the first time.

"I'm thirsty," the man said again.

It was so blatant it took her back. At a distance she could manage him in her mind. Up close his presence was almost too much. But she recovered quickly. "Who isn't? This sun would fry a lizard's tongue."

> *At a distance she could manage him in her mind. Up close his presence was almost too much.*

"Give me a drink!"

"You—a Jew and a man—ask me—a Samaritan and a woman—for a drink?" I have a simpleton on my hands she thought.

"Thirst makes friends of us all," the simpleton said. "I will help."

Before she could protest, he moved the lid off the

top of the well and stood waiting for her to give him the bucket.

"I'll do it," she said.

She let the bucket fall down the well. The splash rang up from below. She swung the rope sideways till the bucket at the bottom tipped and filled. Then with quick, successive jerks she pulled it to the top.

The man waited at her side. He said nothing.

If he thinks he is going to be first, she thought, he thinks wrongly. This is our well and it is my bucket. He will learn who he is here.

She rested the bucket on the ledge, hunched over it and splashed water toward her mouth. She drank like an animal that had been worked too long in the sun. All the time her eyes darted from the water to the silent man at her side. He was smiling. The simpleton has missed the meaning, she thought.

When she was done, she stepped back. The man did not move. She waited, then, finally, jerked her arm toward the bucket. Slowly he cupped his hands, dipped them deep into the bucket, and brought the water to his mouth. As he drank, his face was turned up into the sun and the water ran and glistened in his beard. He drank like a bridegroom, loving the first cup of wedding wine.

With his lips still wet from the water the man turned to her. "If you would ask me, I would give you living water."

"The well is deep." Her tone was instructional. She felt as if she were giving a child a lesson in logic. "You do not have a bucket. Therefore, how do you propose to fetch the water?"

"Yokes and buckets are always the problem, aren't they?" said the man. His arms flew up in the air in exasperation.

A smile popped open her eyes, but her lips stayed tight and disapproving. Not a simpleton, she thought, a child. Just a child.

The child had a question. "Do you have a husband?"

The question slapped across her face. Not a child, she thought. A man, just another man. "I have no husband."

"True enough," said the man. "For you have had, ah, five husbands and the husband you have now is not your husband."

"Do you have a wife?" she spat back.

"I have no wife," said the man.

"True enough," the woman said. "And the woman you had last night was not her either."

The man laughed, like someone had taken him and turned him upside down. He is enjoying this, she thought, but not for long.

"Besides, prophet, the number is not five but twelve."

"I was never good at numbers."

"One for each tribe of Israel," she said and thought that would do it.

"Very pious of you," said the man. "Very pious."

This time she could not catch the laugh in her teeth and swallow it back. It escaped and howled out loud like a prisoner finally free in the sun.

"You are very hard to get rid of," she said, but now she wasn't sure whether she wanted him to go.

"Everyone says that," said the man.

One more try, she thought, and this Jew, like every other man, will surely leave me. "Tell me, O prophet, who is not very good at numbers, where should we worship the living God? On the mountain or in the Temple?"

The man grew silent and closed his eyes. He seemed to be traveling deep within himself to some sanctuary where she could not follow. So this is it, thought the woman. It will be in the name of the living God that he will spurn me.

When the man opened his eyes, he caught hold of the woman's hand. "God is not on the mountain, but in your thirst. God is not in the Temple, but in the scream of your spirit, and it cries to me. Ask me, ask me for a drink."

Not just another man, she thought. Not just another man.

She pulled her hand back. "I don't ask." She said it as if her whole life was in every word.

"Even without a bucket—if you ask me, I will give you living water."

So they sat on the ledge of the well under the sun which shines on good and bad alike. They spoke no words. Finally he reached out for her hand. She let him take it.

"Give me a drink," she whispered.

"What," said the man, "you—a woman and a Samaritan—ask me—a Jew and a man—for a drink?"

"Thirst makes friends of us all," she said and smiled.

The man took her hands in his and formed them into a cup. Together their hands dipped deep into the bucket and brought a cradle of water to her lips. She drank it slowly, with her head back, her face open to the sky. She drank like a deer with the thirst of summer, like a field parched by drought, like a desert wanderer finally at home.

With her lips still wet she said to the man, "Some- times the yoke and

"Thirst makes friends of us all."

buckets cut into my flesh so bad I want to yell with pain, but I never do."

"I know."

Then she told him all about the husbands who were not husbands. She told him everything she ever did. Everything she ever did she told him. All the time she spoke, she cried.

When she was finished, he said, "I know." Then he told back to her everything she ever did. Everything she ever did he told back to her. All the time he spoke, he rubbed the nape of her neck where the marks of the yoke were the most punishing.

It was just as he had finished his revelation of her to herself that she saw the other men. His friends were coming towards them. "They will be scandalized to see me here with you." By now he held her in his arms.

"Probably," the man said.

"I must go." She eased out of his embrace and moved gracefully away from him. As she walked away, she turned often to look at him. Whenever she did, she always found him looking at her. Even when his companions gathered around him, he stood on the ledge of the well and watched her go. Finally, she was so far away she could not watch him watching her.

Then she could not get to the village quickly enough. Once there, she went from house to house and told people about a man who was not just another man who taught her how to drink. It was only after she had stirred up the entire village that she realized she had left her yoke and buckets at the well and for the first time in memory was not thirsty.

The curious villagers formed a circle around her. She stood in the middle and proclaimed: "I met a man who told me everything I ever did—except how many times."

And she laughed high and long. Some of the villagers said it sounded like she had a fountain of living water springing up inside her.

Let those who have ears to hear, hear this story. Let those who have eyes to see, see this scene. Anything can happen at a well.